The Sacred
and
The Damned

a novel

J. R. Klein

Publisher: Del Gato

Library of Congress Control Number: 2025914842

ISBN: 979-8-9923841-4-7

For Democracy

Also by J. R. Klein

"Change will not come if we wait for some other person or some other time. We are the ones we've been waiting for. We are the change we seek."

— Barack Obama

"Never doubt that a small group of committed citizens can change the world. Indeed, it is the only thing that ever has."

— Margaret Mead

Prologue

My father used to say that if I had one failing, it was that I wanted to believe people were basically good at heart. And that, if I had two failings, it was that I wanted everyone to be like me in that way. But, of course, evolution confers on us not just two failings. That much, he need not say. What I have come to learn, however, is that everything we do in life shapes who we are, who we will be. And so now at times there wells up in me a deep and compelling urge to tell this story.

It could be said that my father was a man who was difficult to warm up to, a man on whose face a smile rarely appeared. I liked to think that in him kindled a swath that few saw—warmth that ran deep into the grist and marrow of the man. Thus, I knew that my father was no different from anyone who sets foot on the planet. That there are many people like him, people whose countenance is a masquerade that hides shades of joy or sorrow.

Though he was a man of solid intellect, the fact that he came from barely a middle-class family furnished him with a dose of inner strength and determination that pushed him to succeed in his job as a turner of securities on the Chicago Board of Trade. Five days a week he rode the Burlington commuter from Hinsdale to Chicago. Then upon returning home a tumbler of vodka martinis was swirled with meticulous care and he sat in the living room alone for forty-five minutes.

My mother died when I was eight from what was said to be ovarian cancer though it could have been from some other form of cancer. After she was gone my father uttered barely a word about her. Seeing his lifelong grief, I rarely mentioned her in his presence. He never remarried.

My name is Nick Schefield. As an only child I grew up in an elegant house with my father and a housekeeper and a cook. Left mostly to my own devices, it would be a mistake to say I was unhappy. I had many friends, enjoyed school, entertained a good performance in sports, and by the time I was eighteen had sprouted to a healthy spot just over six feet, if perhaps notably lean and awkward.

1

L ate in summer of that year I left for college. The choice of the school was less mine than my father's. "Bradford University," came the words throughout my early years as though setting the stage for a conclusion that was unlikely to be attenuated. "Bradford University, a good school...my *alma mater.* Of course, Nicholas, you need not study finance as I had done," he would say with tight brow as if the decision to spend a life bartering pork belly on the Board of Trade was barely a thrilling endeavor. Nonetheless, "Bradford it will be" is what I often heard.

The university shared a level of reverence with schools such as Harvard, Yale, and Princeton. Its alumni numbered two Nobel laureates—one in Chemistry, one in Literature—a Secretary of State, a Supreme Court Justice, a tidy number of Pulitzer Prizes winners, and no matter how dubious in purpose and quality, an ever-growing litter of members of Congress.

On the fringe of the campus was the town of Huntington Wells, founded in 1743 by John Huntington. As a young man in his twenties he put a deep well in the ground that gave girth to trees and nourished crops, the nearest river of consequence being the Merrimack. Hence, the name Huntington Wells was bestowed on the small hamlet by neighboring farmers.

Hardly anything had changed over many decades. Narrow cobbled streets laid out centuries ago from ballast stones of tall ships twisted through the village. Simple clean houses and cottages. Tudors of the faculty, deans, and upper administration appeared as the school grew and expanded. A great mixture of stores and shops—restaurants, delis, cafés, pizzerias, pubs, taverns and bars, eight in all, two inns, a tobacconist, a small supermarket, two pharmacies, and a butcher shop—made up the core of the shire. All this acceded to a bucolic stretch of New Hampshire's green and fertile land that tolerated tyrannical winters and held kindly to summers, springs, and autumns. Trees—oaks, maples, elms, and sycamores—clung to deep summer green before turning to shades of red, yellow, purple, and amber as the season prescribed.

The campus was laid out and sculpted in gothic Oxford architecture with an occasional utilitarian blemish appropriately devoted to administration and the like. Those disappointments notwithstanding, most buildings boasted lavish limestone and granite with stained-glass windows of purple, green, red, and yellow that hailed a comforting brew of soft light throughout the interior. Fraternity and sorority houses, though hardly pulchritudinous, held to a motif of Georgian brick that overall did not offend the basic aura of the school. In all, the school gave forth a semblance of scholarship and comradery and independence.

Arriving at Bradford a week before classes, I felt that the choice of the school, though made by the persuasion of my father, was nonetheless a suitable selection for my aspirations. I settled into a dorm room, cookie-cutter by design. A desk, a window that caught a glimpse of the quadrangle, a soft chair, a bed that did not offend, a bookcase, a small refrigerator, a bathroom and a shower, a closet which though hardly large was sufficient. I wasted no time exploring the campus as late August air blew past me in drafts of cooling warmth.

Sampling buildings and halls and centers one-by-one, I pretended I was in Carcassonne deep in the Aude of old France. The library, the oldest structure on campus, was by far the most beautiful. Built from local New Hampshire stone it was capped with a pair of copper cupolas on the top floor above the entrance. Everything about it granted a feeling of harmony and enlightenment. The doors, though taller than me by half, rotated with perfect ease as if I were passing through the portal of a grand and spectacular cathedral. Room after room with stacks floor to ceiling or with long oak tables and chairs bearing a patina from decades of use. I sat at a desk and thought about what the next four years might bring. I was a planner, an organizer, a habit gathered from my father no doubt. I had always constituted my life carefully and, like him, had designed it with a bias toward precision. I looked around the room as rays of the early afternoon sun dripped through the stained-glass windows bringing in a bright and gay glow.

"Yes, here is a place I can study," I said quietly to myself. I wondered who I would meet at Bradford. Wondered, worried you might say, whether I would manage to make friends the way I had done in high school. What would college students be like? Serious and studious all the time? A part of me hoped not. Or would they maintain a fun side as I had managed to do while steering myself through life? It could be said that I did not take all of life too seriously. In that way I differed from my father, a man whose stern grip on the world around him was ever present. I hoped life at Bradford would be good. This, I thought of as I sat alone in the library.

I went to the Student Union and bought a cup of coffee and watched an eclectic coalescence of women—tall and short and blonde and dark and every blend of human alleles—as they passed immune to my presence. I wondered who would become a friend. It brought inner laughter to me. Would one of them become a girlfriend? I played a game guessing who it would be. Music emerged from a speaker. I knew the song and hummed along.

2

So, Nicholas Schefield it is," came a voice as I sat at my desk. Standing in the doorway was a person likely my age though shorter and broader in hips and chest. He wore drab green cargo pants, a plain black t-shirt, and black boots. A short beard shared a hue with a stalk of hair that plumed from his head. Aqua eyes tempered with a dash of gray.

"What is it then? Nick or Nicholas?"

"Doesn't really matter. Mostly it's always been Nick, I suppose."

"Nick Schefield, huh?" he said, putting his hands into his pockets. "Well…either way, it's good to meet you." He crossed the room and offered a hand. "Krause Lunz, here. Yep, Krause Wilhelm Lunz. How's that for a name?" His laugh seemed honest if rather long. "Mostly I go by the name Krause, or more often than not just Lunz. It has a ring to it, doesn't it. Lunz, I mean. You know, like those celebrities who go by one name. Elvis or Sting or somebody. Anyway, if it were up to me, Krause would be fine. But don't be surprised if you hear Lunz quite a lot. It does have a certain ring to it, though. So, where are you from?"

"Hinsdale…a place on the west side of Chicago."

"Thought as much. From somewhere in the Midwest, I mean. I'm pretty good with accents. Could probably have guessed Chicago even though I've never been there. Probably hit every bloody city in America at one time or other. Funny, though, never Chicago. All I know is it's big. My parents dragged us on all kinds of dumb vacations when we were young. Me and my brother and sister. You know, like trips to Niagara Falls and the Grand Canyon…all that stuff. We made the rounds. Oh, we did! By the time we were teenagers they bagged the vacation crap altogether." He made a slow rotation and took a few steps toward the door then came back. "How'd you end up at Bradford? The Brad, I call it."

"My father went here."

"No shit! So did mine. What did he study?"

"Finance. He's a broker at the Board of Trade in the Loop."

"Okay," Lunz abstractly replied. He invited himself to the window and looked out for a second and rested his hands on the sill and stared out a while longer. "Broker, huh?" he murmured, his back to me. "I've even considered it from time to time…you know, the broker thing. Yeah, well…TBH, I'm thinking about something where you can make tons of money…tons," he said, still gazing out the window. "You know, when you see the Brad from a window like this, it looks downright decent, huh?" He angled slowly across the room. "Anyhow, the way I see it, the best thing to do is to get into the club. That's what I call it, the club."

"What club is that?"

"You know, the millionaires and billionaires. Christ, every day a new one of those clowns pops up. The tech rats at Silicon Valley and the hedge fund jocks on Wall Street. Hell, those SOBs make more money than anyone has a right to. And to top it off, you have to wonder how happy they are." He stopped speaking as if contemplating his words.

"Some are, some are not, probably. That's how I see it. I haven't given it much thought."

"Well, I have. And my guess is this. My guess is they're all miserable bastards, the rich SOBs I mean. How many damn yachts can you buy? How many mansions? My guess is they're all miserable as hell. Don't you think?"

"I don't know. You tell me. How can anyone figure out what goes on inside someone else's head?"

"Bet you're planning to be a psych major, huh?" he said, his voice barely hiding an edge of disapproval.

The best I could do was laugh at his sudden intimation. It didn't faze him.

"Well, give it some thought. That's what I'm saying."

"Psychology?"

"Hell *no*. About the rich bastards. Just think about it. You'll understand."

"Well, I haven't, nor do I plan to. And besides, you seem to forget about all the rest of the people who are *not* millionaires and billionaires. Seems you've forgotten about them."

"Ah...they'll be fine," Lunz said, offering little eagerness for the topic.

"Didn't you say a minute ago that you want to make...what was it...tons of money? Is that what you said?"

"Did I? I don't know, it's possible. There's another problem today. See, our minds move faster than we can keep pace with. We're burning out every bioelectrode in our brain. It's a huge problem because we're rapidly becoming nothing but a bunch of torqued out zombies." He watched my reaction. "You think I'm joking?"

"How would I know?"

"Doesn't matter whether you believe me or not. Trust me, it's true."

"Well, I'm no neuroscientist, that's for sure, I know nothing about brain bioelectrodes or any such things."

"Well, I do. I've read extensively on it. You can go to the internet. I guarantee you'll find all kinds of shit about it. All kinds. Let me tell you, the crap they smear us with at places like this, at the Brad, is way out of date. I can see already you don't believe me, do you Schefield? You'll see…eventually you'll see."

"I'm not even sure what you're talking about."

"You'll see…you'll see. Sooner or later all this will sink in. Check it out. There's tons of shit on the internet about it."

"Well, I'm here to go to class and get a degree, nothing more,"

"Every day there's new stuff coming out about how our brains are being turned to nothing but pablum. The information may seem inscrutable but it's not. It's completely true. One hundred percent true and proven to be so." He turned abruptly, his back to me for a moment, then swung around to the room again.

I didn't reply. I sensed more was to come regardless.

"Know why?"

"Know why what?"

"Why our brains are rotting down to nothing. Radio waves, laser beams, wi-fi, the list goes on. See that printer you got there? You go to print a page from it and what happens? The room is floating in a mesh of laser beam waves. They trap our brains. You know, like those porpoises that get caught in the nets of fishermen and can't get out. The whole room is swirling in laser beams. A giant network of invisible vermin that's chewing up every neuronal connection in our brain."

"I suppose you don't have a printer in your room."

"A printer?" Lunz raised a shoulder but didn't answer. "And you know what's worst of all? Cell phones. You might not know it but Bill Gates and Steve Jobs and a bunch of others like them were working for the government from day one. It's a well-laid-out strategy to control what people think. Remember when they used to put subliminal ads on TV? The stuff you couldn't see because it flashed on the screen for a millisecond or two? Trying to get us to buy shit we don't want...or need? It's even worse now because we're buried in an ocean of invisible laser beams. We don't even know what we're getting blasted with. But it's not just what Gates and Jobs did. There's a raft of companies out in Silicon Valley that are contributing to the problem. They're growing up like toadstools in the yard after a summer rain."

"I don't know. Haven't really thought much about it."

"Well, I have and it's a lot worse than people know." He angled toward the door. "Ah...I guess I've pestered you long enough. Want to say it was good to meet you. If nothing else, you can probably see I'm a person with a multitude of opinions. I don't know about you but I think that's a good thing," he strode across the room with the swagger of a prosecuting attorney before a jury. "Anyway, my room is just down the hall. Stop by and we'll bounce some ideas back and forth. *Ciao!*"

3

It was past noon when I went to the cafeteria for lunch. I used the back steps of the dorm so as not to get caught by Lunz on my way out. Surely there was something he had forgotten to tell me, this man of grandiose ideas. What's more, were I to get nabbed passing by, I had a suspicion I would find him printing something on a laser printer. If he were, a series of explanations would likely come quickly forth. It didn't matter. I always had an elastic tolerance for foolishness, a trait probably gifted to me by my father. Or perhaps a residue of goodwill I had picked up from my mother in the years we were together before she passed. A time of which I had little tangible memory.

I looked at the old stone buildings as I crossed campus. The gaping mouths of the gargoyles in permanent guard over the rooftops. The air was sauced with an earthy bouquet of wheat and barley and oats from the fields beyond Huntington Wells as the planet slowly tilted and the stubborn molecules of summer began to lose their grip, reminding me of late August days on the west side of Chicago. If nothing else, Lunz was right when from my window he declared that the school looks downright decent.

The cafeteria food at Bradford was reliably good though it

should be known that I was not the best judge of that given that I generally liked most of what was set before me as a child. And while the cook my father employed put an honest meal on the table, if perhaps somewhat robotically prepared, I nonetheless enjoyed it having frequently wondered what a home-cooked meal, one that came from the pots and pans of my mother, would be like. Therefore, it mattered little what choices were offered in the cafeteria. There was always something sufficient to suit my palate.

I ate my meal, stuffed green peppers, rather dutifully as I paged through the book for my afternoon Psychology class, chuckling quietly when I thought about Lunz's abhorrence for the subject. I had no particular interest in being a psychology major; it was merely a course that fit into my tight first-year schedule. All the same, I felt that I was going to like psychology with its elaboration of how the mind keeps us strung to its whims and fantasies. I wondered if perhaps Lunz might not himself be a psychology major despite the displeasure he advertised for the whole affair. Off and on I had met people like that throughout life. People who eyed how someone would react to an inane proposition. Like setting a face card down just to see who would go for it.

"Hi, Nick. Can I join you?"

I looked up to see Monique Dubois. I had talked with her several times, having ended up in the same Psychology section. I found her uncommonly attractive. A merge of genes from her African American mother and French father. She had a room on the floor below me in the dorm.

"Yes, yes, please, please," I said.

She sat at the table. "The school has a good feeling about it, don't you think? I have a feeling I'm going to like it here. Last year I visited a bunch of schools with my parents. We went to, oh, let's see, to Yale and Hopkins and to Penn in Philadelphia. And to Stanford and Berkley on the West Coast, and a couple of other places. A place I liked a lot was Rice University in Houston. It's just the right size. The campus is very pretty. A lot like Bradford but with a southern feel to it. Eventually I decided I wanted something in New England. When we came here, I knew right away it was perfect for me. It's so beautiful, isn't it? The buildings and all, they have so much charm. I always dreamed of going to college in New England."

I explained that my father had gone to Bradford but confessed that no matter what I would not major in finance as he had done. Crunching numbers held no fascination for me.

"My parents met when they were students at Columbia in New York," Monique said. "My father studied in Paris and then came to the US to go to law school." She wrinkled her nose and shuddered. "I'd never want to be a lawyer…ugh. My mother is from New York. She has a PhD in art history. I love art. I used to talk with her for hours about it. My father works at the Justice Department, and my mother works at the National Gallery of Art. I grew up in Alexandria, Virginia like a thousand other bratty government kids," Monique said with a bubbly laugh. "Living around Washington was all right but I'm glad to be in New Hampshire. The town of Huntington Wells is really charming. Kind of like those small New England villages you always hear about. I haven't seen much of it yet but from what I can tell there are quite a few restaurants and stores and—" She stopped speaking for a moment. "Wouldn't you know it," she groaned. "Look at me…yak, yak, yak…on and on…yak, yak, yak."

"No, no, I love hearing about it," I said. "I've been sort of exploring the campus a little. One of the buildings I like best is the library. It's quiet and peaceful, almost like the inside of a medieval castle. Stained glass windows and all. A great place to study."

I wanted to keep the conversation going but worried that my inherent insecurities with women would prevent me from moving it along. Fearing I would say something stupid I hunted for words. As if perfectly timed, Monique said, "Oh, please call me Mona, that's what my parents and all my friends back home call me. Monique is a nice name, but it sounds so formal to me now.

An hour flew by. I was locked onto every word Mona said. We left the cafeteria and found ourselves sitting on a bench in the quadrangle.

"Let me ask you something, Nick. Have you met this guy Krause Lunz?"

"Krause Lunz? Oh yeah, I met Krause Lunz. His room is down the hall from mine. He's not shy about making an appearance, that much I learned."

"He stopped by yesterday," Mona said.

"Really? What'd he want?"

"I'm not sure. You know, he seemed like one of those people who talks to everyone. I got the feeling he bumps around the hallway until he finds someone he can chug with. He was sort of annoying."

"Did you tell him you were busy, that you didn't have time?"

"Sort of. But I'm the kind of person who hates to be rude. Well, at first he just talked about junk here at the Brad, that's what he calls it…the Brad. Some of what he said was kind of funny. Stuff about various professors. I laughed a little, not knowing who he was talking about. I don't know what year he's in. Third or fourth maybe. I'm not sure. I have a feeling he's going through burnout. That he's tired of school and wants to move on. I've heard it happens to some students when they get close to graduating. Anyway, he talked about some of his classes. He said they all suck and that they're a waste of time and that the professors don't know what they're talking about. That all their information is out of date. He wanted to know what classes I was taking. I ignored him. Well, the way I figured it, he didn't need to come by and pester me with all of it. I mean, cripes, I don't even know the guy."

"Just this morning he kind of floated into my room and introduced himself a little and started clocking on real hard about all kinds of stuff," I said.

"Yeah, all kinds of stuff. Said his parents, his mother and father, are both psychiatrists. He calls them Shrink 1 and Shrink 2 after Thing 1 and Thing 2 in Dr. Seuss's book." Mona simpered. "He said his father went to college at Bradford. That's why he hates psychology. Even though it's not the same as psychiatry he still detests it because it's similar. And he said he doesn't think people have a right to screw around with other people's thoughts and that shrinks used to give people shock treatments to mess with their brains and to get them to forget stuff and that it was all done against their will and that the government approved it, that they encouraged it to get certain people to behave…to get them to do what the government wanted. That's what he said. And then he said all psychiatrists are nuts and he's happy to be away from his parents. And that people become psychiatrists to deal with their own knotted-up lives because they themselves are nutcases. And that normal people never become psychiatrists. Said his parents are both 'looney tunes', those were his words, looney tunes. He went on and on and on for a long time. Kept going and going."

"He told me his father went to Bradford," I said, "but he never said what he does now, never said he's a psychiatrist, and that his mother is too. Not that it would have mattered to me."

"Anyway, I was pretty busy and didn't really care to hear it. But then he settled onto this government stuff and really hung onto it for a long time. It seemed to be something that bothered him a bunch. He became real serious about it. All kinds of junk about the government."

"What about the government?"

"I'm not so sure what he was getting at. It didn't make much sense and it was hard to follow and besides I was busy study-ing…studying *psychology*."

I laughed. "So, he has this thing about the government, huh?"

"Big time. He was really wound up—he complained about everything. I can't even remember it all."

"Was he serious or just screwing around?"

"*Ooh no*, dead serious. I hate to keep the door to my room closed because then I feel so shut in," Mona said. "But I might have to. I've been trying to ghost him but having little success. He keeps coming by. Asks a lot of nosy questions. I have a pic-ture of my mother and father on my desk. He saw it and stared at it for a while and then picked it up and looked closely at it. I didn't say who they were but I could tell he knew. He turned and looked at me, sort of studying me and then looked at the picture again. I was annoyed and ready to tell him to leave the picture alone but he put it on the desk. I figured the less I said, the bet-ter."

"When I left for college, my father told me I'd meet different people of all kinds," I said. "He never said much more about it. I guess he figured I'd know once I got here."

"Funny, but my mother said the same thing to me. She was the person I could rely on for...for...what should I say. She always had good advice about life. I'm an only child and my parent spoiled me, I think." Mona laughed soft and easy.

The conversation drifted back to our classes again. Wayfaring students of all sorts crossed campus alone or in groups. Walking fast and with purpose or slowly as if done for the day. The afternoon sun felt good on my shoulders but most of all I was happy to talk to Mona. The moment I saw her across the room in Psychology I wanted to get to know her.

4

I started reading a chapter in Tangsley's book on American History. The professor was a well-known—famous in fact—historian who sailed through lectures filled with humor and occasional bright and witty flashes of bon mot. Information rolled off his tongue like a well-prepared preacher's homily as he strolled across the front of the room never referring to a note to pace his monologue.

Fragrances of cut wheat and rye from the fields beyond Huntington Wells snuck in the window I had cracked open earlier in the morning. My thought moved to Mona. Skin the shade of mahogany, rust-brown eyes that carried a garland of warmth. She always seemed to be full of happiness and joy. It was not long before my thoughts were shattered by a voice at the door.

"Hard at work? Or am I derelict for coming in and slamming your thoughts?" Lunz said, inviting himself into the room. "You see, when we look out a window, it doesn't mean we're daydreaming...it means we're deep in thought. Bet you didn't know that, did you?" He plunged into a meandering explanation. "Now, it's none of my business, of course. But, well—"

I looked allergically away as he continued to prattle.

"You see, I've been wondering. What makes people come to a place like this? To the Brad I mean? Crazy as it sounds, it's one of those questions that's been bugging the shit out of me all day. Did you ever have that happen to you? I passed all kinds of people when I walked across campus this morning. What a motley conglomerate of flesh. That's when the question got seeded into my brain. I kept wondering: what made them push the default button and come to the Brad?"

"Haven't thought about it."

"Well, I have. And it's important to pay attention to these quirky thoughts that grow from nowhere." Lunz paced in a small circle like a cat waiting to be fed. He stopped and adjusted his gaze on the wall behind me avoiding eye contact. "So here's the crux of the problem, the marrow of the bone, very few people ever fully know why they make the decisions they do."

"So why'd you come to Bradford?"

"Long story," Lunz dismissively replied.

"Well...*do* you know why?"

This time he pursed his lips and gave a sidelong unhappy glance in my direction. "Not hardly relevant. I'm talking more in the generic...the generic. Your question is highly specific."

"Sounded good enough to me."

"We're getting off target."

"I wasn't aware we were trying to solve some earth-shaking imperative."

Lunz shrugged. "And by the way, what is it you're studying so diligently?"

I aimed the book in his direction.

"*Ha,* I had to take that stupid-ass class, too. The one taught by Tangsley...right? The guy's a quack. A complete quack. Famous historian they say. So, what's he doing at Bradford? Why isn't he at Harvard or Yale? Stanford maybe? And all his students are required to buy his book on American history. He's always hocking his book to students. What a grifter! I've forgotten more about American history than hair-brained Tangsley will ever know."

"Seems to know his stuff pretty well to me."

"He's an entertainer, for Christ's sake. A bloody entertainer. Should be hosting *The Tonight Show* or something, not pretending to be a history professor. And watch out, his tests are incredibly unfair. Asks questions about shit he never discussed in class. That way he can give plenty of Bs and Cs. It makes him look like he's a tough teacher. The Brad loves that. Then they can act like the students are working hard for grades." Lunz flossed his fingers through his hair and groaned. "The whole thing is one big damn scam. Let me tell you, this school has it all figured out. They dupe the students into thinking they're getting a hotshot education."

"Well, we haven't had any tests yet," I said.

"Just wait, you'll see. I know every one of their tricks. I could write a whole manual on it. But why would I? I'm not here to bail out all the witless SOBs who come to the Brad. They're going to have to figure it out themselves. I'm just giving you a heads up, Schefield, because you seem like a pretty decent guy. Not like most of the other dorks here. Anyone whose father moves pork bellies around at the Board of Trade can't be all that bad."

"How kind of you, Lunz."

"We know why you came to the Brad, and why I came here, I suppose. That good old legacy crap thanks to our fathers. But mostly everyone else got tricked. Universities are great at it. They have a bunch of people who go out and peddle the school like it's a falafel sandwich or something. It's all a big goddam game. And it's not only at Bradford. Oh, no! No, no! Even those glorious schools like Harvard, Yale, and Princeton—Hopkins, too. They all do it." Lunz waved his hands back and forth like he was shooing a mosquito.

"I don't see what's wrong with it."

"Here's what's wrong." He stopped speaking as if rummaging for what to say then blurted, "The problem is this…universities are supposed to be institutions of higher education. Take the great schools of the Middle Ages, for example. Oxford, Cambridge, The Sorbonne in France. You don't think they went out foraging for students, do you?"

"I think you're trying too hard to conflate the two—the school and who goes to it and how they got there."

"Conflate. Ha, good word, Schefield! *Good word!* To conflate: to join, to bring together," Lunz said as though offering a definition at a high school spelling bee. He walked toward the window and circled back.

"So, am I to conclude then that you're an English major?" I said.

Lunz huffed but didn't answer. "I have another one for you. Question, that is."

"Thought we were talking about why people come to Bradford."

"We are…I suppose." He turned to me and said, "While we're at it, have you met the two chicks who share a room down below?"

"I've met almost no one. I've only been here a short while."

"Holly Clarke and Jennifer Rubinstein. Holly's a sophomore. We know each other very well…*ooh yes, we do*," Lunz said, in words that carried biblical implications. "So, you haven't been down there, huh?"

I shook my head. I found the question odd.

"You should get to know people," Lunz said, sounding like advice that might come from my father. "Well, let me tell you. Holly Clarke, she's a nymphomaniac. A goddamn nymphomaniac. But a damn good looking one," he solicitously added. "So, anyway, we screw around a lot, me and Holly. And like I said, she's a nympho. Can't get enough of it. She started coming up to my room because she didn't want us balling in her place with Rubinstein coming and going. And before I knew it she was in my room almost every night...and every day. That woman has more mones flowing through her than everyone at the Brad together. Wow, she's fire! Not sure why she wants to share a room with a bagel like Rubinstein."

"What's wrong with that?"

Lunz glanced to see if I was serious. He started to say something, then backed off and said, "Actually, I have to admit it, Rubinstein...I'll bet she's a real torch, too. Pretty goddamn good looking for a...you know, for a—" He crossed the room and stood at the window and viewed the campus for a while. "There's a lot of them here at the Brad...Jews. I know the Ivy League clubs are packed with them but I didn't think it would be like that out here in lily-white New Hampshire."

"What do you think the school should do, put limits on who gets in? Is that it? Go back to the good old days?" I said, framing the words in quotes with my fingers. "Is that what you want?"

"Balance in the school body is...you know...is a good thing. When it gets out of hand it causes resentment. You might not know it but lots of the plebes here at Bradford are aware of it and don't like it. See, when students come here they think they're coming to a nice quiet Anglo joint. And then they get hit with Hanukkahs and Yam Kippurs and dudes wearing yarmulkes and all the rest of that shit."

"What's it to you, Lunz?" I said. "You know I don't think you believe any of this. I think you're just a provocateur who likes to piss people off. That's what I think."

"Believe what you want, Schefield," Lunz mumbled.

"And, while we're at it, you never told me what your major is," I said.

"Don't remember you asking."

"Just did."

"What's yours?" Lunz said, redirecting the question.

"I don't have a major yet. Won't have one until next semester. Maybe not till next year. But I bet you're a psych major, aren't you?"

"*Psychology!*" Lunz roared, his face erupting into a bloom of vermillion. "Do I look like a goddamn fool? *Do I?* Let me tell you something, no normal person would be a psych major. Know how I know? Huh? Know how I know? Both of my parents are psychiatrists. That's right, goddamn psychiatrists…*psychologists* with a prescription pad. That's what shrinks are." He left the window and thumped into the room. "Went to medical school and couldn't find anything *proper* to do so they smashed the escape button and came out as shrinks. Get a load of that, *goddamn shrinks!* What an embarrassment. Like the world needs another shrink, right? Like we don't have enough mind benders and couch surfers already?"

"Okay, fine," I said, wanting to back away from having unwittingly led Lunz into a rant.

"What I'm telling you is, some things should never be taught at universities. Being a psych major makes about as much sense as…as being a PE major. Give me a freakin' break! Does anyone really need to learn how to be a jock, for Christ's sake? Cut it out! If I were president at Bradford, I'd yank both of those right out of the curriculum. And a few other ones as well. Sociology. There, fling that one, too. What the hell is a sociologist anyway? About as relevant as a being a shrink."

"So, your parents are psychiatrists, huh?"

"Yeah, yeah, yeah…psychiatrists. My mother, Shrink 1, is a child psychiatrist. My father, Shrink 2, does depression stuff and junk like that," Lunz said, his voice now almost calm. "Pushers, both."

"Pushers?"

"Pills, dude, pills. That's what shrinks do. They keep their patients so chemically waterlogged they can barely think straight: addies, roxies, special K, xannies, the list goes on and on. Half the people in this country are pumped full of meds for depression, the other half is packed with stuff for attention disorders and everything in between."

"Your parents told you that?

"Have you ever been to a shrink, Schefield?"

"Not yet."

"Do you know how many psychiatrists there are in the US?"

"Can't say I've checked."

"Some forty-five thousand. Know why?"

"Are we playing twenty questions?"

"The government, that's why."

I shook my head and looked away.

"I can see you don't believe me."

"Cut it out, Lunz. I have no idea what you're talking about now."

"The government, dude, the government."

"You're not suggesting the government controls how many psychiatrists there are, are you?"

"Look it up. It's all right there on the internet. It's how the

Deep State controls everyone. Don't believe me? Go check it out."

Lunz could tell I was finished with the conversation. Glancing at his watch, he said, "Okay, maybe this is a good time for you to get back to Tangsley," he said shaking his head in disgust. He left and clunked on down the hall.

I worked on history for a while and then set the book aside and spread out on the bed and stared at the ceiling. Lunz was becoming a true pain in the ass. Maybe I should shut the door as Mona suggested. Yet, he wasn't the first of his kind I had met. Going to a large suburban high school I found myself ricocheting off all kinds of mortal bombasts. Some of whom filled the classrooms with inanity, while others were iconoclastically bright in their own way. Which was Lunz? I had heard that children of psychiatrists unwittingly spend their formative years on the couch as it were, though I had no firsthand evidence of this. Was it possible that Lunz had received a double dose of it, a homozygous rendering throughout his years at home? Poor guy. But then, what did I know about such crap? Nothing. So, I couldn't tell if Lunz had acquired his irksome attitudes in childhood or if he was camouflaging himself in a weird game of hide-and-seek. I thought I had the tools to handle a person like Lunz. Now I wondered.

5

I had just opened a book that was assigned in English Literature when Mona appeared at the door.

"Got a minute, Nick?" She sat on the bed and put her hands on her knees. It was clear something was bothering her.

"Mona, what's the matter?"

She drew in a breath, exhaled, looked away for a moment then turned to me and said, "Well...I was in the hall outside my room talking to Jennifer Rubinstein. We were minding our own business, talking about our classes and then—"

"And then Krause Lunz came by."

"Uh-huh. I left right away and went to my room but he followed me. When I got there he shoved me into the room and started to close the door. I told him to stop and ordered him to get out. He was in a real bad mood. It was frightening. I told him to leave but he wouldn't go. He kept staring at me, looking all over me. Then for no reason he started talking about Holly and Jennifer. He said he's known Holly for quite a while. I don't know why but that's what he said. Then he went into a long tirade about the government. This time he said the government has gone way too far and that lots of people are fed up. He was very hyper, almost as if he was on some sort of…really wired. I told him I had no idea what he was talking about. He tried to explain but when he saw I had no interest he said something real creepy. He said my room smelled different from the other rooms—Holly and Jennifer's room, for example. I always keep my room clean…I mean super clean. That's the way I am. I've been like that my whole life."

"Maybe that's what he meant."

Mona shook her head. "No, he didn't mean that. I know he didn't. He didn't mean it in a nice way." She started to say something and stopped as if hunting for the right words. "I know exactly what he was getting at. Lunz knows I'm part African American. I told you how he was studying the picture of my parents that I have on my desk when he was in my room the first time. You might think you get used to the, oh…the nasty comments. The innuendos." She shook her head. "But you don't. You merely learn to live with them. When people say stuff like what Lunz said, they always try to make it sound like, what should I say, like it's something that just spontaneously came to them, that it means nothing. I knew *exactly* what he meant. I knew exactly what he was saying. In fact, he probably wanted me to know. Then he started to really unload. He said when the right kind of people finally get control of the country, they'll gather up certain groups and send them out. It doesn't matter whether they're citizens or not. The people in this country, the ones who are the problem, will be removed. Locked up in detention camps and then sent out. He described them like they were lice on a dog or something. He was all fired up, very adamant about it. Talking fast and almost screaming. Even said it will be like what the Nazis did to the Jews. He kept staring at me, real sick like."

Mona stopped for a second and dried her eyes and said, "He kept going and going. On and on about how it won't be long before the country takes care of the problem the way the Nazis did in Germany. He swore it was going to happen. I told him he's crazy and then he got even more angry. I mean *really* angry. He waved his arm and said: you just wait. You wait, it's going to happen. It's going to happen. It was clear who he was talking about…the people that need to be removed from the country. He didn't fool me even though he never actually spelled it out, not in so many words. I tried to get him out of the room but he stood there and kept going non-stop. And then he started talking about junk he gets from the internet. He said there's a lot of good stuff for anyone who wants to see it and that people shouldn't believe what they see on the news because it's fake, totally made up, but people watch it and believe it. He said it's all rubbish. I didn't know what to do. I pulled my phone from my pocket. He must have thought I might call security because he turned and stormed out."

I told Mona to lock her door if she ever saw him wandering by her room. She got up and started to leave. I pulled her to me. "Oh Nick, I'm sorry," she said. "I didn't come down here to tell you this. I'm sorry." She rested her head on my chest. "Why is this happening? I came here to get an education. I thought it would be fun. That I would make lots of good friends. And I have. I've made some really good friends already. And then this happens. I feel so sick inside." She kissed me on the cheek and left.

I did not see Mona for two days. I worried that she might have left campus. That the incident with Lunz might have driven her to quit school at Bradford. Twice I went down to see if she was in her room. The door was always closed. Jennifer Rubinstein said Mona had not left and said she was spending most of her time studying at the library. I ran into her as I was coming across campus.

"Oh, Mona, I was worried that you left Bradford," I said.

"No…I was just in the dumps for a while, that's all. I'm better now. But about the other day, I didn't mean to act like a child. And no matter what Lunz does, I will *never* let him destroy my life. Never, ever," she said defiantly."

6

Returning from the gym, I had just stretched out on the bed as Lunz came flouncing in.

"Sound asleep, eh? Did I wake you? A nap at midday is good for the heart, they say."

"Piss off, Lunz," I said, going to my desk.

"What's stirring inside Schefield today?"

"Were you down in Monique's room?"

"Monique?"

"Yes, Monique. You know who I'm talking about. She has a room next to Holly Clarke and Jennifer Rubinstein."

Lunz shrugged. The look on his face said he was searching for a way to lie his way out. "I talk to Holly Clarke now and then, so what?"

"I asked about Monique."

Unexpectedly, Lunz said, "Sure, I know who you're talking about. The Black chick on the floor below, though I'm not certain she's *completely* black. Not totally. Not a full one hundred, if you get my point. Not fully baked, you might say. Didn't really ask her but you can tell just from looking at her that there's not much dark chocolate there...more like mocha. Means there's been some serious jumbling of chromosomes. But it's not a surprise really. Blacks and whites have been shagging each other since the first one came from Africa back in the sixteen hundreds or whenever—"

"You were rude to her, Lunz. Not just rude but you insulted her."

"Oh really, O'Reilly. When was this?"

"You know when. Two days ago."

"I don't know. Maybe I talked to her. I talk to lots of people. What's the big deal?"

"You said some pretty disgusting stuff to her."

"Did I?"

"You know damn well you did. Keep your racist attitudes to yourself."

"So, who are you, her guardian angel?"

"Fuck you, Lunz. Quit harassing Monique."

"Take it easy, dude, take it easy."

"Leave her alone."

Lunz looked toward the window but said nothing.

I was planning to get Lunz out of my room when he suddenly entered inchoately into a rambling diatribe as if every word of our previous conversation had flown straight past him. I was struck at how easily he did this.

"I didn't come down here to get into a big tug-of-war with you, Schefield. Here's what's new over my way. A spanking new laser printer. Yeup, a new printer," he said in an awkward voice as if he had artificially dreamed up the topic on the spur of the moment.

"Thought they burn holes in our brains."

"Ah, ha, ha. See, Schefield, you need to learn how to take

what people say with a grain of salt. I hope you don't believe everything you hear. That won't get you far in life. Assuming that's your *goal*," he boorishly added.

For a split second I wondered if this was a cryptic warning not to take seriously every word that came from his mouth. Perhaps telling me he was merely trying to fuck with me. Showing me that he himself did not believe much of what he was saying. That it was all a game on his part. Maybe he was just an outlandish flake and I was letting myself get sucked into his outlandish game.

He moved toward the window and angled back. "Okay, fact is, I did originally say that. But see, I hooked my printer to an Ethernet cable. *That's* the difference. Not sitting in my room being tazed from all over by wi-fi beams that are slowly burning holes into every millimeter of my gray matter." He waved his hands frantically like he had just walked into a spider web. "That's the difference. You see, the government wants us to toast our brains. They're trying to turn us into a nation of sheep. On fleek—there's a good book for you, Schefield. *A Nation of Sheep* by William Lederer. Ever read it? Doesn't matter."

"What the hell is all this government paranoia, Lunz?"

"Jesus, Schefield, what planet are you from? You need to get up to speed, dude. Like quick! I can give you some sites to go to. Social media joints and other places. Facebook, even. I know all the good ones. I can point you in the right direction."

"You know, Lunz, I don't have time to go poking around in those. Is that what you do all day? Read the garbage that's on the internet? Sit around and read that crap? Is that it?"

"There are lots of good sites on the internet. Sites with information from people who know what they're talking about. If you knew the ones to go to, the pages with the *real* shit, not the spin that comes out of the Deep State, you'd be enlightened. You'd stop drinking the Kool-Aid Bradford serves."

"And you came in here to *enlighten* me. Is that it, Lunz?"

"Hell no, Schefield. You can stumble through life on your own. Why the hell do I care? However, there are some great reads on the internet I could direct you to, out of my inherent benevolence, of course."

"Save your fucking benevolence, Lunz."

"Someday you'll want to know. Just wait." He ventured into another jumbled rant. This time about my history class. "What's Tangsley up to now. Drumming on about the slave crap, I bet. The guy Spends way too much time on that shit and not enough time on the important parts of American history. He knows he can scrub off an entire fucking lecture, a whole week in fact, on that and not utter a meaningful word…it's easy drift for Tangsley. But what do you expect from a lazy SOB like him? That shyster's always looking for ways to tweak his way out of giving an honest lecture. The students don't realize this, of course. They say: Wow, ole' Tangsley really knows his shit. This is what you get when you have a classroom full of people with minds that are little more than Silly Putty."

Everything was beginning to come together. The comments about Jennifer Rubinstein and Mona, his endless tirades about Bradford, his paranoia about the government. I no longer thought of Lunz as a provocateur as I once believed. Though I knew there were people who espoused wild beliefs of all kinds, I did not expect to collide with someone like him at Bradford.

He dove into a rant about the evils of interracial marriage, a topic that brought out one of his darkest sides. Trying to cut him short I made the foolish mistake of asking what his problem is with interracial marriage. With refueled choler, he said, "It's not *my* problem. It's the *country's* problem. Truly hard to believe you're so far behind the eight ball. On the one hand, you've got the Jewish elite running the country. Got their hands in damn near every aspect of it. Banking, of course! That goes without saying! They've been doing it for centuries. Why stop now? Even our old buddy Shakespeare knew all about it…take Shylock in *The Merchant of Venice*, for example. Shakespeare knew what the Jews were up to way back then. He was trying to warn everyone who had a whit of knowledge…"

"So what's it to you? What do you care? And you left out Shylock's conversion to Christianity at the end. I guess that would not fit into your worldview."

"It was a bribe, Schefield, a goddamn *bribe*. Read the fucking play."

"All right, let's forget it."

"And they run practically all the media in this country, too. And damn near half the professors here at Brad are Jews. You haven't figured that out yet, huh? Well, it'll become abundantly clear soon enough. They love jobs like this—being a professor, I mean—when you consider how easy it is and what lazy bastards they are."

"So, I guess I can add antisemite to your list of wonderful qualities."

"These are facts, Schefield. Facts!" His voice swung high. "This country was settled by Christians on Christian beliefs, and Christian scriptures, dogmas, and principles. Christian. Get it?"

"The country was settled by American Indians on what *you* would probably call Pagan principles. You seem to have

33

conveniently overlooked that."

"Yeah, yeah, yeah, and look what happened to them. Got themselves snuffed out in pretty short order, didn't they? Oh yes they did. Oh, yes."

"Because they were not Christian, is that it?"

"Democracy is a hoax," he continued, shifting gears. His words rolled out like a misguided version of a Tangsley lecture. "Most Americans haven't figured that out yet. Clearly, *you* have not, Schefield."

"Last I checked, it's worked for over two hundred years."

"**C**ut *the crap, Schefield!* That's such bullshit. Do you know why? Do you? Because it took…how long…a damn long time for women to get the right to vote in this country, and for Blacks and others to get equal rights. But don't think I believe Black folks should have equal rights. In fact, for all we know Monique might be here because the Brad, the leftwing flophouse that it is, opens its doors to all sorts of people even if they're not qualified, not up to snuff so to speak. Fortunately, the geezers at the Supreme Court nipped that one in the bud, didn't they? Yep, every now and then the Court knocks one out of the park. A grand slam. Not often enough, but sometimes. They certainly did it when it came to affirmative action. Even good old Stepin Fetchit Clarence Thomas voted to scrub affirmative action despite the fact that he squeezed his big black ass into Yale Law because of it. Not saying Monique doesn't deserve to be here…so don't get pissed, okay? Just saying the whole process has been a huge, gigantic, colossal catastrophe."

Seeing that this was quickly moving from bad to worse, I was ready to inform Lunz that I was busy and that I had other things to do. Sensing my mood, he unceremoniously left.

I stared at the book on my desk. Even with Lunz's emotionally destructive visit, I had managed to carve out a solid morning of studying. A gentle rain began to sprinkle the window with shiny droplets as if to cleanse my room of the scum of Lunz. The air blowing in carried the smell of moist grass and damp earth. It reminded me of similar days in the Midwest that spoke of autumn, telling you that summer was packing up and on its way south. I was looking forward to the kaleidoscope of the oaks and sugar maples as the days grew shorter and cooler.

I thought about what I would be studying during the next four years. I was not sure what I wanted to do in life but I was certain what I did not want to do. Medicine had a certain appeal to me. The ability to have an impact on a person's life. Conversely, I had no interest in being a lawyer. The mere thought of it curdled my blood. And I knew with certainty that I had no desire to be a wheeler of soybeans, corn, and wheat on the Board of Trade as my father had done his entire life. But there were scores of other tantalizing ways to make a living. Something in government perhaps. Despite what some people might believe, people like Lunz in particular, I felt that working for the government could be rewarding. I especially liked the idea of going into the diplomatic corps. My father had a close friend who had been the Ambassador to Turkey and had worked at numerous other embassies. When he stopped by on warm summer days to share an extra dry martini with my father on the back patio he always took time to describe his work to me. It sounded exciting to live in a strange or exotic land and work with interesting people. The sort of job I could enjoy. One of my inner strengths, one that was evident to all who knew me, was my capacity to tolerate people of every ilk. Witness Lunz. Which of course was not to say I could not be provoked at times. Yet, interestingly, it was in my DNA to hear people out, to listen. Was this what made for a good diplomat? I had no way of knowing.

Lying on the bed, I thought about the courses I might take to move me in the direction of government service. Which would I need? History of all kinds, some philosophy, anthropology perhaps, foreign language. Maybe even a course in communication. It did not really matter; the university would dictate the slate. I laughed when I thought about Lunz's reaction if I were to tell him of my tentative plans.

I went to the cafeteria for lunch. The choices were fine. Besides the typical fare of burgers and sandwiches, they offered a variety of hot lunches. All the usual suspects I had grown up with as a child. The predictable but tasty home-cooked food that even a university cafeteria could not destroy. I scanned the menu and settled on Swiss steak, mashed potatoes, vegetables, and a slice of apple pie. I thought that perhaps I should have invited Mona to join me for lunch. It was clear that my thoughts were always drawing me to her. To her infectious smile and joyous laugh.

Lunch was certainly no worse than what had been prepared in Hinsdale by our cook. My memory of those days brought nary a moment of homesickness. I was happy to be away from the well-honed routine my father had carved out for himself. I never held it against him. It was his life, his routine, not mine. Even so, my new unfettered life as a student blended well with my psyche.

As usual, I was early for Biology, a class that was held in a large lecture hall with tiers of seats that permitted unobstructed vision to the front of the room. I took my usual place toward the back of the room—the classic choice for a semi-introvert. Chatter filled the hall until at exactly two o'clock as precisely as when the clock at the *Gare du Nord* ticked onto the minute for the train to depart, Professor Grayson entered and placed himself behind the podium. There was no need to call the class to order.

"We left off with the oxidative phase of glycolysis," he promptly said. "PGAL, which we discussed in the last lecture, has a low-energy bonded group attached to it…" He turned and drew the equation on the whiteboard in a rapid manner, making a correction by erasing the improperly placed hydrogen atom. "If we get another phosphorylation, say from phosphoric acid in the presence of DPN, the net result is diphosphoglyceric acid and from this…"

He talked in a quick, bold, staccato voice, moving across the front of the room, sometimes with head down as if addressing his shoelaces, then immediately directing his attention onto the room with eyes that focused on some abstruse point beyond us. He paced across the front of the room never losing the continuity of his words. His arms raised and his head bobbed as he talked. Walking to the board, he rapped on it with a persistent and emphatic knuckle to emphasize a point. There was an uncanny stillness in the room. Heads moved up and down—some up, some down like a choppy sea. At other times in unison in one great swell. The lecture continued uninterrupted for an hour and fifteen minutes at which time the board was covered with numbers, letters, arrows, and geometric figures as well laid out as an intricate tapestry yet somehow resembling a child's random scrawl.

The second Grayson stopped, students snapped their books and laptops closed and edged through the rows. I left the hall feeling invigorated, intoxicated. For the first time in life I felt genuinely happy. The years I spent in Hinsdale now seemed strangely inadequate, unfinished. How odd it is that we develop a different view of events as we move forward as if the present and the past are only tangentially connected. Do we distort our memories of the past, and if so, why?

I hoped my enthusiasm would carry me through my days at Bradford and that I would not dull to the pedantry of learning. I wondered if this was what had happened to Lunz. Was he suffering from scholastic burnout as Mona had suggested and now had turned on us the venom of what filled him? A dilemma: should I shut him out of my life, close my door and stick a BUSY sign on it and turn myself into a Carthusian monk? Or was I being brutish to myself for even letting Lunz's behavior cloud my thoughts and my time? Well, of course, I was.

For two days I did not see Krause Lunz. No sudden appearances at my door. I surmised he had ventured off in search of others to torment with his endless prattle. Or perhaps he actually had work to do, schoolwork. Something he hardly ever talked or seemed to care about.

7

I slept late Sunday morning. All my life I hated getting up if I didn't have to. As you might expect, my father was an early-to-bed, early-to-rise person. A routine that fit well with his life of vodka martinis, stirred and never shaken, and never more than one a day except on the rare occasions when someone as important as the Ambassador to Turkey stopped by. I often wished I knew if my mother's daily routine was as closely pruned as my father's. In the world I had invented of her, I preferred to believe she was more like me when it came to the little habits we acquire in life.

I got up and made a cup of tea—floated a bag as I liked to call it. Sitting in my chair, sipping tea, the skeletal remains of a dream came to me. Krause Lunz stood on a wooden box like an old-time politician. Arms waving and body gyrating in clumsy motion. With each thrust of his shoulders he cried out and moaned and blasted forth a litany of words, none of which I remembered. His eyes were ablaze. In front of him was a vast lawn of people transfixed by each word. Now, he was in the quadrangle at Bradford proclaiming that the time had come…it had arrived. He bellowed a psalm of angry words as students listened in rapt silence.

The dream faded. I ran through my plans for the day. Some time ago I remember reading that the Dalai Lama said the first thing he did each morning was to define his goals. I liked that and had done it for many years. I would work in the morning on my courses and prepare for the week's lectures. Tangsley's class was daunting, but so were Grayson's biology lectures. He, especially, managed to deliver an incredible amount of material in an hour and fifteen minutes twice a week, much of which was new and difficult to grasp. I plugged my way through the textbook page by page reading many times what Grayson had covered in his blitz of rapid-fire lectures and chemical diagrams that filled every inch of the board with little effort on his part. Yet I mostly liked biology, difficult as it was, though I was not sure how it fit into a career in government I was beginning to plot out.

After a morning of non-stop study I opted to take a walk. I could have left by the back steps but looking down the hall it appeared as if the door to Lunz's room was closed, thus sparing me an encounter with him on my way out. I snuck quickly by but as you might expect I was nabbed.

"Schefield, Schefield."

My body turned mechanically toward the partially open door. I stood motionless like a petty criminal, a shop lifter caught in the act holding a package of Twinkies.

"Schefield, enter…enter," Lunz said in an unusually congenial voice.

I took a reluctant step into the room.

"Where to, guy? Where are you off to on this beautiful Sunday?"

I told him of my morning of study hoping it would be

sufficient to satisfy his curiosity.

"Too nice a day to piss it away with your nose in a book."

His room was cut exactly as mine. Identical in every way but for Lunz's choice of decoration. On the wall was a large flag. Red with a white disc and a black Iron Cross.

"Lunz, what the hell is *that*? What the hell is it doing here?"

"What is it, you ask? History, dude, history. An Iron Cross. Nothing more...."

"What do you mean, nothing more! Do you think I'm some kind of idiot?"

Lunz rocked in his chair. A look of delight lit his face as if he joyed in having raised my ire.

"It's simply a military decoration used for many centuries in Prussia...and Germany, of course. That's what it is. That and nothing more. You see, my roots, ethnically, go back to that region. And proud of it I am." This led him into a rambling and disjointed diatribe. "Therein lies the problem, Americans have no history. Or if they do, they have forfeited it, given it up, or more than likely, have no idea what it is. People in this country don't know Shinola about who they are. All they know is the garbage they heard in the second or third grade. Most of which is total bullshit. But there...there," waving a finger sharply at the flag, "*those* people there did not lose sight of their past. Not like in this country where people have thrown away their roots. But take a gander—some of us have not forgotten. Some of us know exactly where this country came from and where it should be going. So, you see, *that* piece of historical beauty on the wall is a reminder of what this country needs to do, what it must do."

"You know, Lunz, it's Sunday. If I wanted a sermon, I'd have gone to church."

41

"Churches are for people who can't think for themselves," Lunz growled. He clasped his hands behind his head and said, "How's Monique? Saw you two coming across campus last night."

"So?"

"So, nothing. Anyway, I was balling dear old Holly Clarke most of the night. But later we went over to the ratskeller for a beer. I thought I saw you two coming back this way, that's all. Didn't know you guys are a thing, you and Monique," Lunz said, an odd ring of jealousy in his voice.

"We were coming back from seeing a play at the theatre department. And before that we had pizza at Ponzo's in Huntington Wells, if you need to know..."

"*Fat Ham*, I saw the notices about the play. Something about a dude at a picnic down south or whatever. Hamlet redux if I got it correct. Doesn't sound like much fun to me...not the way they pegged it."

"Keeping track of folks now, huh? What the hell are you...the SS?"

"Ha, ha...funny, funny, funny, Schefield. See, that's the problem, you think I'm a Nazi or something. Don't you?"

"Are you?"

"You already asked that."

"And you never answered."

Lunz got up and bent forward and stretched and went to the window. He pulled the sash up. A wave of fresh air entered as though eager to get in. It carried all the fragrances of early autumn as each day cast itself farther from summer. Lunz leaned forward on the sill, then stood and deposited his hands into a pair of cargo pants of the kind he always seemed to wear and took in a breath of air. He rolled his shirt to his elbows and returned to the desk.

Glancing about the room I noticed he did not seem to be studying. I couldn't tell what he was doing, his desk was positioned with his computer open to the wall behind him. On the corner was a bevy of pill containers and bottles of what appeared to be vitamins and assorted medicines though I was unable to identify any from where I stood. None of that mattered. I had no interest in knowing what Lunz was up to.

"What do people say when they see that flag of yours?" I said.

"The flag? Nothing."

"Nothing?"

"Holly Clarke asked about it once but never said anything more. All she knows is how to get laid. And that, she knows how to do damn fucking well! Excuse the pun."

I shook my head. I was getting ready to start for the door when Lunz said, "Well, seems as though you've become quite familiar with Monique. Where'd she get that name, Monique? Holly told me she goes by Mona. Cute, but I sort of prefer Monique. Not bad looking for a, for you know—kind of reminds me of Irene Cara. Remember her, the black chick in the movie Fame?"

"We're in a class together, nothing more.."

"Let me guess…psychology."

I said nothing.

"That's a yes, probably," he said. "So, what's she like? Monique? I've always wondered about it, you know—" Noticing how his question bugged me he let out a crude laugh and pushed onward. "Always wondered about that. Yeah, always wondered. What I heard is that black chicks…they're…you know. You know what they say about black chicks. Probably a vestige of the days they were on the plantation when the dude in the big house was humping his little Mandingo honies. Not that I really approve of it, mind you. The black-white thing, the…but we already went over that. What say we don't dig it up again."

"What say we don't."

"Well, you can see where this country is headed. It's rotting from inside. It started after the war when we let Jews in by the boatload…."

"Are we going there again, too?" I said.

He continued unfazed. "Tons of them cram-packed into steerage. I told you where that led us. And then, of course, along comes this hick from Texas…LBJ. Look at the shit that happened after he pushed all the civil rights garbage through. But the *biggest damn mistake* this country made was putting Obama in the White House. From then on, it's been nothing but trouble. You might not know it but lots of people—and I mean lots, tons of people—tried to warn us what would happen if he became president." Lunz stopped speaking. His brow curled as if some devious thought had come to him. He turned to me and said, "While we're at it, Schefield, you wouldn't perchance be a Jew, would you?"

"Why do you ask?"

"Schefield, that's why. Name sounds kind of Jewie to me. Even Nicholas could be Jewish. Jews like to give their kids names like that. Don't always name them Mort or Sydney or Melvin or whatever." He searched for other examples but came up dry.

"You're a fucking asshole, Lunz." It was clear he was hunting for buttons to push. He already saw my reaction to the Iron Cross on his wall and his comments about Mona. It was evident how it delighted him, how he had drawn immediate satisfaction from my reaction. The morning was too nice to destroy; I let him plug aimlessly through his tedious sermon.

"Let's say I was Jewish, Lunz. Just suppose. Okay?"

"Then you'll do absolutely fine here at the Brad. Hell, I could probably fix you up with Jennifer Rubinstein. Wouldn't that be sweet? I bet she's good in the sack. You can look at someone, and you know it's true. You can get a mental picture of them knocking their damn brains out or whatever. That's how I feel about Rubinstein. She's got that glimmer in her eyes that says she knows all the tricks. I might even jump on her myself if I ever get the chance. Hell, I'm not proud I wouldn't be surprised if she's a nympho, a perv, just like Holly Clarke. For all I know they could both be a couple of dykes. It's entirely possible. I think Holly might be. I got a feeling that door swings both ways. Just a guess but probably true. Could easily be. Got the same feeling about Rubinstein. See, that's another problem," Lunz said, digressing again. "Gays, lesbians, yada, yada. Add in the minorities and the trade unions and you have the whole bailiwick. See what's happening? There are lots of people who feel this way. Tons of people."

Lunz portrayed a crazy vision of one of Hitler's Brown Shirts. A Storm Trooper ranting wildly at me. The cargo pockets he wore were eerily reminiscent of the breeches worn by the SA tucked snugly into jack boots. Shirts with flaps over the chest pockets. All but the shiny leather belt tight around his waist and over his shoulder. The swastika arm band. The salute. The arm leveled straight out and forward. Or aimed awkwardly back over his shoulder at a deranged angle.

"The tide is coming and when it arrives it will clean the

beaches and wash away every speck of rot and detritus that contaminates this country." He said he was writing a long treatise that would explain everything.

"You actually have schoolwork to do after all, huh?"

"Fuck no, Schefield! One more semester and I'm out of here. I almost never go to class. Besides, I can barely stomach listening to the crap they try to get us to believe here. All I ever do is go in and find out when the next test will be. I don't need to listen to their crap to pass their screwball courses. For one thing, not trying to brag," his face broke into an egotistical smile, "but I'm a goddamn genius. Have had to deal with that all my life. Hardly ever studied. Never had to. My classes are an absolute bore. Pure hogwash. It's a treatise for…let's just say an organization I belong to. I've been working on it for…I don't know, for a while. Just about done, in fact."

He described some of it, most of which I had already heard in his pontificating homilies during his journeys to my room. The need to root out the evil that burdens American society. The people who were the source of the problem. He didn't identify the organization he belonged to except to say he knew the government had an eye on them but that it didn't bother him because the government was watching all of us. He didn't care. He said his group had more people than the government had "feebies", his word for the FBI, and that his group was growing by the day. He yawned and said, "Enough of that shit. Holly's coming by this afternoon. Said so anyway. Even after last night, it wasn't enough. Hard to believe anyone can be so goddamn horny." He let out a ghoulish laugh and then in one of his hyper motions grabbed a thick stack of papers on his desk and held it up. "When this baby gets published, the country is going to take a hard right turn, let me tell you. I'll let you read it when it's done, Schefield. Finally, you'll be enlightened. And when you are, you'll want to join our group instantly. I know it."

I gave up. On my way out I turned and said, "While we're at it, Lunz, *you* wouldn't be Jewish, would you?" I couldn't resist.

Lunz's face flushed plum red. He slammed the stack of papers on his desk and stood up. "Do I look like a Jew, do I? Jews all look alike, act alike, talk alike!" He tilted his head down and rubbed the top of it. "Do you see a yarmulke here? No! You are definitely one naïve sonuvabitch, Schefield. One naïve sonuvabitch!" he said, in little less than a shriek.

I went for a walk and found myself sitting on a bench in the quad wondering whether Lunz was truly serious in what he said. His words were so strident, so gross at times, they reminded me of the manic taunts uttered by a carnival barker waving a cane. Tricks to get us to go along with something we knew was a waste of time: "Venture in and witness for yourself all forms of human malformations. Be the first to see it."

Lunz was not the first person like this I had known. There had been others along the way though perhaps lacking his dark view of mankind. Of course, my ever so arcane psyche provided me with a means of accommodating Lunz's off-putting behavior. Let it be said that if there was one part of me I wished I could do away with, it would be that part. Or was it that, perhaps, I should be grateful to have it at all? So be it, I'm stuck with it, I told myself.

8

I did not see Lunz for several days. Sunday afternoon, Mona and I rode our bikes to Samuels' Park. A lush and tranquil spread of green grass on the edge of Huntington Wells. Shady, with a clear shallow stream that bubbled through. The weather was warm with a nip of coolness. The smell of crisp autumn leaves filled the dry air. Mona packed a picnic lunch consisting of a baguette, salami and ham, lettuce, cheese, an apple and a pear, and a large bottle of Perrier. We spread a blanket on the grass and set the basket of food in the middle.

"Let's see what the stream is like," Mona said. "It looks refreshing. If it's not too deep we can wade in a bit."

We walked to the bank. The water trickled across as clear as if it had bubbled up from an underground spring. Pebbles and small stones glistened in the stream. I scooped a handful of water. "Eeyow, it's cold," I said.

"It's not very deep and there is not much current." We took off our shoes and socks. "You first," Mona said with a gleeful laugh. "And then you can tell me what it's like."

"But what if I go and you chicken out?"

Mona chuckled. "Oh, I would *never* do that. Okay…I

48

suppose *I* could go first. But what if *you* chicken out?"

"Cross my heart," I said, almost believably.

"Here we go." Mona reached for my hand and led the way. She took a dainty step into the clear water and pulled her foot out. "Whoa, it's cold. Look, look at the little fish darting about. I love seeing fish like that. They seem so happy in the small piece of earth they occupy, don't they? I had a fish tank in my room back home. I loved to watch them scoot around in their tiny little world."

We ventured slowly into the water and walked along the shore barely to our ankles. An old man on the other side sat in a canvas chair and smoked a pipe as he watched a yellow and red bobber wiggle in the stream.

"It doesn't feel so bad now, does it?" Mona said.

"I can't tell, my foot is frozen."

Mona chuckled. "Come on, let's go a little more along the shore."

Warm rays of midday sun came through the trees. It was good to be away from campus, granted a pardon from hours of studying. We sat on the bank to let our feet dry.

"What a terrific day," Mona said. "I haven't been on a picnic since…since…oh, I can't even remember when."

I said, "I vaguely remember going on picnics with my father and mother when I was little. I have this memory of her being a very happy person who loved to do things like that. Go on picnics and that kind of fun stuff. And I remember going to baseball games with her and my father. Cubs games at Wrigley Field. My father is a big Cubs fan…the Cubbies. It's one of the few times I remember being with my mother. Yes, it's great to be here today."

We grabbed our shoes and went to the blanket. Mona told me about the emails and texts she got from her parents—at least one every day. "I love to get them. I can almost hear my father's voice in the words as I read them. He still has his French accent. It's so melodious, the way he speaks. Everything he says almost sounds like a song. I used to try to imitate him when I was little, thinking my friends would believe I had come from France as he had." Mona's laugh was sweet and happy. "But, of course, I couldn't do it…not the way he does."

We made sandwiches and had cheese and fruit and Perrier. The afternoon continued to warm as the sun rolled across the sky. I stretched out and leaned on my elbow. Mona sat cross-legged near me. Just being around her was a festival of mirth. She ran her finger down my cheek and rested it on my lips. A thrill bubbled through me like the water in the stream. She leaned forward and kissed me on the lips and then looked up at the sky. "Oh my gosh, I'm sorry," she said in a foolish apology. "I…I don't know. I don't know what got into me."

I pulled her gently toward me and kissed her passionately. We sat in what seemed like perfect silence. As I began to speak, I saw a bike coming down the path. The rider looked lethargically in our direction then turned a second time and set his eyes squarely on us. He brought his bike to a stop. I could tell immediately it was Krause Lunz. He stared for a minute or so, then took his phone from his pocket, and aimed it at us. It was obvious he was photographing us. He stared a while longer and then mounted his bike and sped off.

"Is everything okay?" Mona asked.

"Yes, it's fine," I said.

She turned and looked behind her as the person vanished in

the distance. We lay on the blanket facing each other, talking until late in the afternoon.

That evening as I sat in my room I kept thinking about Lunz spying on us in the park. *What a goddamn nosy bastard. What a nosy bastard. I'm damn sick of him prying into my life!* I paced across the room. *Should I tell Mona that I had seen Lunz watching us in the park?* I hadn't mentioned it to her at the time. I was sure she could not see him from where she was sitting. I did not want to ruin the good time we were having. *Well, maybe I should tell her now. But what would it do? It would only confirm what an ass Lunz is and we both know that all too well. No, I won't tell her. I'll go down and confront him directly. That's what I should do. Demand to know what he was up to. That's the right thing to do…isn't it? Demand an explanation from the bastard.* I paced across the room again and then sat at my desk and tried to focus on my Monday classes, hoping that would sate the anger that was swirling through me. Of course, it did not. Five minutes, ten minutes, twenty minutes.

I got up and paced the room. Pulling my thoughts together, I walked down the hall, stopped halfway, started to turn back but continued on to Lunz's room. As always his door was partly open. He was typing at his desk, oblivious that I was standing in the doorway. Looking up, he said, "Well, guess what? It's Nicholas Schefield. And what brings dear old Nicholas Schefield here this evening? Come for some enlightenment, did you?"

"Cut the enlightenment crap, Lunz."

"Oh, and I can see we are mad," Lunz said, leaning back in the chair.

I glanced about the room and pulled in a slow shallow breath and exhaled. Seeing the large flag with the Iron Cross did little to calm me. "Yes, Lunz, I *am* pissed," I said, after a short while. As he waited for me to speak, I noticed for the first time a bleak emptiness in his face. A vague and coddled expression he kept well hidden. A coldness that seemed to come from some dark spot deep inside. Odd that I hadn't noticed it before, but there it was. I aimed an arm at Lunz, finger pointed acquisitively. "You're right, I *am* pissed. I want an explanation and it better be good. What the hell were you doing spying on us this afternoon?"

"On you? You and who?" Lunz asked, raising a brow in mock confusion.

"Cut the crap, you know what I'm talking about!"

He leaned forward, elbows on the desk. "Fill me in, Monsieur, I am clueless. Mind reading is not a strength of mine. And here I am working feverishly on my treatise." He stretched his arms over a passel of paper.

The more he joked, the angrier I became. I was tempted to cross the room and leap at him. I realized that every encounter I had with Lunz was a form of torture.

"Today when I was out in Samuels' Park in Huntington Wells. That's what I am talking about."

Lunz looked toward the ceiling and squinted. "Hmm." He closed his eyes as if attempting to retrieve a lost memory. "Huntington Wells, Huntington Wells. A beautiful little burg, wouldn't you agree?" he said, striking each word ponderously and evenly. He grasped the edge of the desk. "If nothing else, we here at the Brad are lucky SOBs just to be near Huntington Wells right here in the great state of New Hampshire, the Granite State." He let out a crusty laugh. "Huntington Wells, named after some limey who put a well into the ground way back when…how inspirational. How—"

"Shut the fuck up and listen to me!"

"Your turn to speak."

"I was in the park minding my own business on a picnic with—"

"Let me guess…with Monique."

"*Yes*…with Monique, yes. I saw you photographing us. Do you think I'm blind or something?"

"Do I think…or *did* I think? There is a difference. I can probably rule out blindness morphogenically in as much as you did not stumble your way in here with a cane to guide your steps. So then, that leaves us with the other option. *Did* I think you were blind…"

"Goddammit, Lunz, *answer the question.*"

"I'm trying to. I'm trying to."

"Why were you spying on us?"

"All right now, let's get to your question. First, you assumed that this person who was spying on you, as you imply, was *me*. Do you know that for sure? Well, do you? How close was this person to you? Five feet away, ten feet away, a hundred yards away? Second, how do you know the person was taking pictures of *you*? People take pictures of all kinds of shit when they go to the park. Don't you? Well? Birds, trees, flowers, all kinds of shit."

"You need to mind your own damn business," I said. "Mind your own damn business and stay the hell out of mine. Monique is a wonderful person. I'm sick of you poking around in our lives."

"You know, Schefield, I think you just ruined a perfect Sunday. I was just about to crack a beer with a couple of buds. Toss the pigskin around. But you just tanked the whole goddamn day."

Too annoyed to say more, I turned and walked sharply out. Returning to my room, I grabbed a coffee cup from my desk and threw it against the wall. I sank into my chair and swung my feet onto the ottoman, eyes closed. My heart ran fast, the adrenalin that flooded my body, pumping hard through it. I placed two fingers on my carotid. More than a hundred and going like fire-hose driving a gush of blood through me faster than the water in the stream in Samuel's Park. I slowed my breathing, hoping it would help. In, out…in, out. Think pleasant thoughts. Get control. Think of the stream. The happy guppies that darted about without a care in the world. I thought of Mona—the tightness in my shoulders and the muscles in my back and neck began to release. I felt disgusted that I lost my temper. Me, a person who rarely lets his emotions get the best of him and yet once again Lunz had succeeded in tearing apart the issue I went to confront him with. He was good at that. The more I mulled it over the more I realized that the points he made could have been true. Perhaps he was not the person in the park. Well, perhaps he wasn't. Perhaps it was someone else. Someone who did not even know me or Mona. It was possible that I was wrong about Lunz spying on us. A poor calculation on my part. Was I firing missiles at an imaginary target? And let's not forget, Lunz never said he was in the park at all. Should I just forget the whole affair? Lunz had a way of casting me as a bungling fool. He was damn good at it and I was damn good at letting him do it.

Not ten minutes passed before Lunz was at my door looking calm, hands in his pants pockets. "Got a minute?" he said coolly.

I did not reply.

"Okay, I could see you were pissed when you were in my room a minute ago. It was plenty evident." Lunz came forward a few steps. "You thought I was spying on you. But given that we share the same dorm, the same Hobbit hole you might say, I figured it is to our advantage to stay on good terms…why not, eh? So here are the details. You see, I was balling dear old Holly Clarke most of the afternoon. Afterward, we decided to go for a bike ride, just like you and…just like you guys did. We rode through the park and then headed out beyond Huntington Wells. But from what you told me this person who stopped and took pictures of you was done by himself. True? So, you see, it could not have been me because I was with Holly, and from what you told me about where you were, we were nowhere near you. We were all the way on the other side of the park. There you have it." He shrugged and flounced out of the room.

9

We sat on a bench outside the library. The air was warm but not hot, cool but not cold. The kind of day that boasts of autumn. We laughed at what the psychology professor, who always spiced his lectures with wit, had said.

I was getting ready to tell Mona of my encounter with Lunz the night before when she said, "I talked to Holly Clarke this morning. I guess she knows Lunz pretty well. She said something I thought was sort of crazy. She said Lunz showed her a tattoo he recently got. It was a set of numbers on his right forearm. Holly wasn't surprised by it, not too much. People have all kinds of tattoos these days all over their bodies. Well, everyone but me. I'm aiming to be the only person on the planet without a tattoo." Monique chuckled. "So, Holly didn't see what the big deal was, but Lunz said he just recently got it and that it had very special meaning. He told her it's connected to an organization, a group of some kind that he belongs to. Said he would tell her about it eventually, that it drew its meaning from World War Two, but he didn't say how. All she knows is that it is some sort of radical political group."

I thought about the flag with the Iron Cross that Lunz had

on his wall.

"He also told her he's going to be away for a few days to a convention with this group of his, a special convention of some sort. They're going to make plans for a big event they'll be holding. The only reason I mention this at all is because Holly said she's beginning to get a bad feeling about Lunz. She said she liked him for a while...even found him sort of good looking. She told me they had sex a couple of times but she didn't like it all that much because he was...well, she didn't say why. All she said was she thinks he doesn't have a good opinion of women. She didn't elaborate. And she said he keeps ragging on about how certain people have screwed up the country and that they need to be stopped before it's too late. He's said that to both of us, to you and me. It's clear he has an obsession about how the country needs to fix its problems and do it soon. Holly said he's getting more wired up about it all the time. He let slip what this group of his is all about, from what she could tell it's pretty far right-wing, very fanatic, just like he is."

"Has he been by your room?"

"No, not lately. Maybe he got the message."

"Well, I had a pretty big blowout with him last night." I told Mona what I saw Lunz doing in the park. How he stopped and might have taken pictures of us. I told her I confronted him about it later that evening and how he came to my room and explained that it could not have been him in the park. Mona said she didn't believe his explanation. She heard from Holly that he's been stalking people and that he's getting more paranoid all the time.

"When I confronted him he swore he didn't do it," I said. "Now I feel bad about the whole affair. I'm trying to get along with the people in the dorm. My father always called me: Mister

Go Along to Get Along." I laughed a little. "I used to hate it when he said that but it's sort of true. It's a pretty good description, I think."

Mona said, "This morning I passed Lunz on my way to class. He had his backpack and seemed to be heading off campus. He didn't look at me though I'm sure he knew I was there because he said, 'Hey sweetie, how's your little lover boy? Heading over to put a smile on his face, I bet.' I stared at him. He just kept walking."

"The guy is a damn sterk," I said. "Best to stay as far away from the dude as possible."

"I need to tell you something else, though. Holly told me she heard from one of the girls in the dorm that Lunz went into my room."

My jaw dropped. I uttered something, I don't remember what.

"She might be right, I don't know. Sometimes I leave my room unlocked when I go out. I know I shouldn't do it but…well, anyway, the person told Holly she saw Lunz slip into my room. He didn't think anyone saw him, apparently."

"What was he doing?"

"Holly didn't know. I don't get it. When you come down to it there's nothing worth very much. You know, books, clothes, that stuff. Holly said he wasn't in there very long. But when he came out he had his phone in his hand. Holly thought he had taken pictures. Now I'm *real* creeped out. I feel like he has some kind of obsession with me."

I suggested we report it to the dorm monitor or to campus security. Mona, afraid it would turn into a fiasco, didn't want to. We decided to let it go, figuring there was little we could report except for what we heard from another person.

We left it there until later in the day when Mona sent a text asking if I would stop by her room. When I got there, she was standing over her desk, hand covering her mouth. She picked up a copy of *To Kill a Mockingbird* she was reading for her English class. Her hands trembled as she opened to the middle of the book and retrieved a sheet of thin cardboard no bigger than two inches by three inches: red with a white circle and a black swastika inside. Not an Iron Cross, but a swastika. Classic in shape and design. On the back below *Sieg Heil,* the words, The Day is Coming, were written. She handed it to me. I blanched in shock. Mona turned away then reached for the card with both hands as if to tear it up.

"No, no, no!" I said, pulling it from her. "Don't destroy it! It's important!"

"I'm so scared I can barely think straight." She hugged me tightly. "It's from Lunz, isn't it?" she said. "That's what he was doing in my room. He's the one who put it here. He's a Nazi, a neo-Nazi. The first time he was here I sensed the hatred in him. I could feel it just looking at him. Oh my God, now what? Off and on in my life I've dealt with people like him. My mother was good at helping me with that. I miss my parents a lot."

We sat on the bed. I grasped Mona's hand. She looked at me and swept a tear from her eye. "It's from Lunz, isn't it?" Mona said again. "That's why he was in my room."

"Don't ever go out and leave your room unlocked. Even if you go just down the hall."

"Uh-huh" She dried her eyes and said, "Oh Nick, I came here to go to college and get an education. I had great hopes that it would be a wonderful experience. I like school. I've met a lot of great people, but now this happens. Oh, God. It's as if Lunz has poisoned my whole life." She rubbed her eyes. "We've got a psychology test on Friday and I can barely think straight. Oh, God, I'm so nervous."

"We'll study together. You'll do fine."

We spent long hours preparing. When Friday arrived, we were totally locked in on the test. Even before we got our grades, we knew we had torched it.

I did not see Lunz again for over a week. It was a blessing. I spent most evenings with Mona, studying or listening to music or going to the Union for a burger with an ever-growing number of friends. I aways did well in groups. I was the one who could laugh at any joke no matter how mundane. Mona's effervescent personality was an effective foil for the designated talker. Every group had one, it seemed. They kept the tone and mood of the group alive and fueled the conversation. And, of course, every-one loved the humor of Bobby Ruggles with his litany of satire, burlesque humor, and near-perfect imitations of the faculty.

10

Life without endless interruptions from Krause Lunz was a gift from the Magi. I was in my room listening to a song by *Hem* on a pair of small speakers when I heard a knock. I assumed the respite from Lunz I had been granted was about to end. Looking over, I saw a fellow student in the doorway. Five eight perhaps. Burly with a generally healthy physique if somewhat rotund in the middle. A loft of hair sprang from his head. He wore pants of the color and style preferred by Lunz and a drab t-shirt.

"Hi, how are ya?" came words in classic New York slant. "Howie Berman…dorm monitor," he said as he stepped into the room.

By now I had heard of Berman and his role as dorm monitor though I knew little of what the job entailed. Berman wasted no time in explaining what he did, most of which appeared to be minimally important. All but for one thing.

"I just try to keep the peace…well, as best I can. Let me tell you, it's no easy task, this dorm monitor thing, I mean. No easy task. Okay, it's not like digging ditches or something. It's just that dealing with people can be a real pain in the ass. Not saying I'm good at it…not bad at it either. Takes a lot of what you call your people skills I guess you could say…working with lotsa different kinda folks, I mean. If the sounds get too loud somewhere, it's up to me to get them turned down a bit. And I'm not talking about the good stuff, not chords like your stuff from *Hem*, I mean—"

"You know the group, huh?"

"Oh, yeah. Good tunes…good tunes. I'm from Brooklyn, they're homies. Anyway, it's the loud stuff, the rap and the grunge. That's the crap I hate the most. Can't stand either of them. I don't know which is worse. Grunge maybe. Yeah, grunge probably. I have no interest in that preachy crap that came out of Seattle or wherever. But this much I know, people like to bang the music. Like way up. Like a trillion decibels. You can hear it all over the place once they light it up. I'm sure I don't have to tell you. Makes my job a big freaking scrimmage all the time. Or if there's a lot of turnt going on in one of the rooms, for example. You know, brewskies or whatever." He pantomimed as if chugging a beer. "That sort of thing. It's against the rules in the dorms. There are plenty of places to crack a beer…the Union, off campus, yada, yada…the frat houses, sorority houses…what do I care? Or if someone's burning leaves in their room, you know, puffing a doobie. Or let's say we have someone who plumbs the halls of the dorm bugging the shit out of other people, if you know what I mean."

The cryptic reference to Lunz was not so cryptic. Yet, it was clear from my brief five minutes with Berman that he was no match for Lunz, the bulldozer who rolls over everyone in his path as I already knew from my own experience.

"So, you know Krause Lunz, huh?"

"Krause Lunz? Oh yeah. Sure, sure. Of course I do. Who doesn't?"

"Well, you need to keep him on your radar," I said. "He circles through the dorm like a pissed-off hornet. Comes in here all the time uninvited. If not me, he's always shading someone here in the dorm. The guy has no respect for anyone."

Berman pulled in a breath, exhaled, and groaned. "Lunz is a perfidious fleck. My eternal challenge. Don't forget, I'm not Frank Serpico, I'm just the dorm monitor. I have no way to control a schmuck like Lunz. No one does. I've known him for a while. Personally, I find him to be an emotional wreck…but that's his problem."

"He's got some really outlandish crap in his room," I said. Berman had to know what I was talking about. The Iron Cross, and all. I assumed Berman was Jewish, though I had no cosmic knowledge of that, just a rational guess. He shrugged and adopted a view of the window. Sighing full and deep, he said, "Well, people can do what they want with their rooms. Like I said, I'm the dorm monitor not the interior decorator." He angled around. "We might not like Lunz's wallpaper, as it were. And let's face it, seeing garbage like that cuts deep to my core. But it's not in my purview to rake on him about it. If you want to hang long black curtains in here, who am I to say you can't? Well, there it is. You can see this dorm monitor thing—not much too it, really. Lotta smoke but not much fire. Kinda sucks."

"I have a good idea that Lunz has been finding his way into the rooms of some of the girls when they're not there."

"Really? Who?"

"Some of the rooms on the second floor."

"Rubinstein, Holly Clarke, Monique Dubois? Them?"

"Nice guess," I said.

"Well, like I said, I'm not a member of the Fraternal Order of Police. They'll have to take that up with admin or something."

"Just keep an eye on Lunz. He's a genuine…well, you get the picture."

Berman's head bobbled three or four times. "Yeah, yeah, sure, sure. Look, my plans are to drop out of this dorm job crap pretty soon. Fuggit, what do I care? Planning to tell admin I'm done with the whole freaking thing. More damn trouble than it's worth. Had about all I can take. Besides, it won't be long before I float my way out of Bradford for good. Done here and glad of it," Berman said, sounding almost like Lunz. "Already got into a couple of good Meds and waiting to hear from a few more." He apologized for bothering me and went on his merry way.

Weird cat, I thought, returning to my books.

11

The next day I was working in my room when Lunz appeared like the Ghost of Banquo and looking every bit as inviting. I could tell he was charged and duly stuffed with attitude. I was about to brush him off and direct him to the door when he said, "Probably wondering where I've been, right?"

"Not a bit."

"So here it is. I was at a convention, you might say. A special convention. A meeting of brilliant minds. These are the people who will cleanse this country of every scintilla of evil and mismanagement. While we're at it, take a look at this." He rolled up his sleeve and proudly displayed a tattoo on his right forearm. A string of numbers. Six in all with a line through them. "Got this baby the other day. Know what it is? Go ahead, Schefield, take a wild stab. Of course, I don't expect you to know, given your scant knowledge of world history."

"You came in here to waste my time with a goddamn tatt?"

"Oh, for Christ's sake, Schefield, what does it mean?" He shook his wrist in my direction as if I hadn't seen it. "What does it mean? That's the question. Take a close look."

I refused the bait.

"All right. History lesson. And I don't mean the kind that dribbles out of Tangsley's mouth. I don't mean that. If you go to the internet you'll find all sorts of crap about the Jews in the *so-called* concentration camps being tatted when they arrived. Of course, it's all bullshit. Absolute, total, complete bullshit. The internet is filled with that garbage to get people to believe the Holocaust, as they call it, that it really happened. Well, it didn't, and of course anyone with a functioning frontal lobe knows better. It was a trick created by the Jews to allow them to get into the good schools and to get the good jobs and to make us all feel sorry for them. You know...too bad what happened to the Jews. Get it? They're great at digging sympathy out of people. Look how well they managed to turn Palestine into the State of Israel in 1948. Nice trick."

Lunz continued.

"This here, old boy, is a symbol of my group. Take a good look. See, it's on my *right* wrist. The people who dreamed up the lie about this pretended the tattoos were on the *left* wrist. But we do it on our right wrist. The line through it is symbolic of the hoax, that the tattoos never happened. The Holocaust was a full-blown hoax. All of it is a gigantic fabrication. I can give you the internet sites to go to. Sites that will prove to you what bullshit it is. Sites that detail why the Holocaust never happened, that all the crap about the Holocaust is the real conspiracy."

"That's garbage, Lunz! Total garbage!"

Lunz was unfazed. "But people like Tangsley and all the other clowns in Bradford's ridiculous history department continue to pump the Holocaust crap into the heads of students day after day. That's right, here at Bradford. This lovely institution of left-wing propaganda and poison." His voice leapt an octave, eyes wide. He was in full form. "We're going to erase this crap from the minds of the people in America. My group will do it. You'll see. Just wait. You'll see, and when we do—"

"What group?"

"The group? Is that what you want so desperately to know about?"

"Why are you afraid to tell me? This group you talk about endlessly but won't say who they are. From what I heard, you even mentioned it to Holly Clarke."

"Holly Clarke? *Her*? She doesn't know shit. By the way, did you screw Holly while I was gone?"

I pushed the question off with my hand.

"Should have seized the opportunity, dude. She'd have put a great big smile on your face. That much you can count on. It wouldn't have mattered a bit to me. The thing with Holly and me is pretty much kaput."

"What's this nefarious group you belong to? Afraid to tell me?"

"Not a bit. Soon as I have my treatise done, I'll give you a copy. And when I do that, I'll tell you everything. Won't be long now. Won't be long. But I can give you a few hints. Already did, in fact. Already told you some of it when I showed you the tatt. And at our meeting this week we covered a lot of important shit. Tons! Planned out a strategy to deal with everything. It's all about to come down soon. And when it does, get ready, lots of people are going to be shocked as hell. In fact, when we finally take control, people like you are going to have a plenty to worry about," Lunz said, shaking an angry finger in my direction.

"You're one sick sonuvabithch, Lunz"

Lunz slopped himself into the chair and parked his feet on

the ottoman.

"Were you in Mona's room?" I said.

"Who," he asked spontaneously.

"Mona."

"Mona? As in Monique, you mean?"

"Yeah, yeah, Mona."

He shook his head.

"Were you?"

"Schefield's playing guardian angel again."

"Were you?"

"No, Lieutenant Columbo…satisfied?"

"Someone left a card with a swastika in her book."

"Oh, and you think it was me?"

"Was it?"

"*I…already…said…no!*"

I could almost have believed him were it not for the blush of guilt that filled his face. "Stay the fuck out."

"Jesus Christ, calm down, dude."

It was clear Lunz was not about to confess. "This mystery group of yours—"

"Still pushing that, huh?"

"Know what, Lunz? I don't think the group exists. Maybe you're hallucinating."

Lunz yanked himself forward, shoulders back. "Why do you think I got this tatt, for Christ's sake?"

"We dug through that two minutes ago."

A long awkward silence. Lunz looked at his watch. "Okay, maybe it's a good time to pay a visit to Holly Clarke."

"Thought you said it's over between you and Holly."

Lunz stared at the ceiling and in a subdued voice, said, "Ah,

Christ, we're a damn sorrowful lot. Most blokes tumble through life hoping not to catch themselves on a trip wire. That's about all they want." He started to speak but stopped short as if his words took him a little too close to home. "I know what you're thinking. You think I was stung by my parents."

"You brought it up."

"It's easy to read what's tumbling through that feeble little brain of yours, Shefield. Well think again, fella...think again. I was too smart, way too smart, to get caught in their trap. They knew it and couldn't do squat about it. It is true, however, that most people by the time they're seven or eight have been laid low by the sword of their parents, no one escapes. Every agglomeration of protoplasm that rambles across the planet is caught. Yes, you too, Schefield. You and Rubinstein and Mo—" He stopped abruptly and said, "And Holly Clarke. Her for sure. Surprised you didn't jump her bones while I was gone. But none of this is important. All that's important now is what's going to happen. The day is coming and when—"

"You're not going to lay some goddamn end-time crap on me, I hope. You're not some kind of prepper, are you? Not really into that shit."

"Get with the program. I'm talking about when we take power. My group. Already big as hell and growing by the minute. All the details have been worked out and the rest is up to the people."

"And who exactly are these...these *people*?"

"Every bonehead in this big stupid country, that's who. Every joker who thinks voting is a noble thing. What a fucking lie that is. *What a dirty trick.* They're merely playing in the sandbox of democracy. But here's the hook. People are sick, I mean truly sick of the goons and crets who run this country. The old geezers. It's been like that for a long time and the people are fed up. And so, you see all we need to do is let the people do it for us. They'll get rid of those bastards once the people get riled up enough. They'll accept any freaking alternative. Any! People want someone they can believe in. A difficult challenge for me and my group because this country has been brainwashed into believing that democracy is good. But we've got one thing on our side. Voters in this country are stupid as shit. Do you think they listen to what candidates are telling them? Fuck no! That would require some real thinking. They don't give a damn about policy. They don't know what policy is. They want someone to tell them what they already know—that they're getting screwed twelve ways from Sunday. They know that *everyone* running for office is lying to them. They want the best liar…that's all."

"Pretty morbid thought."

"Not really. A truly morbid thought is that people actually believe that democracy is a great and noble thing. That's what they were taught in civics class in the third grade or whenever."

"And you have something better?"

"Of course we do. Of course, we do. Christ, you must think I'm some sort of dunderhead, Schefield."

This brought great laughter from me and with it a look of disgust from Lunz as he helplessly watched me rock gleefully.

"I can see you don't believe me."

"Never said I did, never said I didn't."

"Sure you did. Just not in words, that's all. When you were raised by two miserable shrinks like I was you learn how to read people."

"You're quite the sorcerer, Lunz."

Lunz grinned, he seemed to like the accolade. "What this country needs is fascism pure and simple. Fascism is a good thing, a damn good thing," Lunz said, parking a hard stare in my direction. "It's the best thing that can happen to a country, especially a country like America. Most of the dunces in this country think fascist rulers take over countries, that they steal control of power, rip control of the country from the hands of the people. That's the bilious that idiots like Tangsley and his lot dish out. The kind of sermons he gives from his holy pulpit in front of a pack of naïve freshmen—his sacred congregation. But nothing could be farther from the truth. Nothing! Good fascists get their power from the people. It happens when a country hits rock bottom and its sacred political systems have failed in every way. Take Mussolini, you might call him the father of fascism, not Hitler like most people think. Mussolini figured out that fascism was the goose that laid the golden egg that he was seeking most of all. The country was flat broke. The people could barely feed themselves. The little Italian runt saw instantly what needed to be done. And a damn good job he did. Of course, it did not come easy for him. And ole' Adolph knew the tricks too, just like Mussolini did. In 1933, the German people elected Hitler to be Chancellor. That's right, *elected.* The country was bobbing around like a rowboat with one oar. The people were ashamed of having lost the First World War. Humiliated, in fact. Hitler learned most of his tricks from the little Dago. Bet you didn't know that the famous salute Adolph brandished, the stretched-out arm thing, was lifted right out of the little Wop's playbook. It's true. It's well documented."

"For Christ's sake, Lunz, I really don't give a shit if it is or isn't. I don't worship the scum of history the way you do."

"What I'm talking about is fascism. Hitler had a solution for the problems of his country."

"Let me guess. Genocide. Wiping out every Jew in Germany. Some solution."

"Hitler knew who was to blame for Germany's troubles. He knew damn well."

"Now I get it. Everything is beginning to crystallize now."

"Don't be so cock-sure, Shefield. It's evident that you've got a lot to learn if you want to find the truth."

"You're a Nazi. Just say it. Come on, just say so. Are you afraid to? That Iron Cross on your wall. What about that? You don't have it for historical reasons or whatever. And the tattoo you came in to show me, what about that? You didn't get that because you think the holocaust was a hoax. You got it because of it's a connection to the Third Reich."

"When people go back and look at the history of the world, an unvarnished history I mean, when they finally do that, it will become perfectly clear that fascism is where it's at—"

"You live in a goddamn fantasy world."

Lunz curled his fist into a ball and shook it at me, a troublsome likeness to Hitler standing on a platform thirty feet above a crowd screaming his fiery words to a fear-drugged audience. "Yes, Fascism! Uncle Sam is on life support, maybe even dead already. Get with it, Schefield. Do I need to remind you that all the great leaders of the world were fascists? Franco in Spain. Lenin and Stalin. Pinochet in Chile. Marcos in the Philippines, Tito in Yugoslavia, Ceausescu in Romania, Gaddafi in Libya. Hitler and Mussolini. Chubby little Kim Jong Un in North Korea. All great fascists who did great things for their people. Leaders who led the people out of darkness. Fascists!"

"Torture, concentration camps, gas chambers, incarcerations, executions."

"Maybe. But don't delude yourself into thinking those things haven't happened here in the glorious U. S. of A...in America, the bastion of freedom." He shaped a pair of parentheses in the air around freedom. "It's worked great for lilywhite people like you and me, Schefield. And for anyone with tons of money. But sooner or later the house of cards always crumbles. And right now the house called America is falling fast. Fascism will put an end to it. Fascism will fix it. Don't believe me? Go ask your little sweetheart Monique how Blacks have been treated for the last three hundred years in this wonderful democracy. Go ahead, see what she has to say about democracy."

"You need to keep her out of this," I ordered.

"Take it easy. Take it easy. And besides, don't get to thinking I'm feeling sorry for them, Black folks I mean. Don't think that! Fascism has solutions for every malady. Fascism will fix every problem in short order. But in this country the so-called solutions have themselves become the problems. Case in point, the Great Society crapola of that yokel LBJ. Any fool with a gram of gray matter knows how it screwed up everything in the whole damn country. It seeded a permanent layer of hatred into it. When we have a person like Mussolini or Hitler or Franco or Pinochet or any of the others running the show, hate will become obsolete because it won't be tolerated."

"That's *bullshit*, Lunz! There was plenty of hate among the German people for the Jews. *Plenty!* The Nazi's didn't eliminate hate; they fed on it."

"LBJ had a plan and it worked perfectly. He got JFK knocked off..."

"No, no, not that now! Nobody believes that crap."

"Look at the facts. The big ornery Texan needed to get Kennedy out of the picture. Notice that he wasn't anywhere near Johnnie-boy when they shredded his skull with the 30.06 that the gang had targeted onto his noggin. The Texan didn't want to get caught with a stray bullet from one of those. Then, once Lyndon was running things, he pushed his program through. The Great Society crap. What a bad joke that was! He knew it would send the country into an eternal boil because it would give Blacks and a shitload of others privileges that would piss off whitey. That's what the Texas hayseed wanted. He knew that all the southern states that had been solid Democrat for decades would now become Republican. LBJ was nothing more than a Republican jiving as a Democrat to get elected to office in Texas. Don't believe me. Look at how well it worked. Look at Texas today. Louisiana, Mississippi, Bama too, Okielahoma, Arkansas. All the same. Red as can be. No Democrat can get elected there to save his soul. Thank you, LBJ. Y'all did a rot good job, y'all did."

"I think you've fallen off your Thorazine, Lunz."

"Fascism will be the final political wave for this country. Countries evolve just like everything else on this planet. And like all evolutionary processes they move to a point of greatest and most perfect harmony. Fascism is the final stop for America because there will be no need for a constitution or courts. The Supreme Court will be the first to go. No need for that. Nothing but a bunch of cantankerous old farts."

"And your group knows who this person will be who leads us to the promised land, I suppose?"

"In time, in time." He checked his watch. "Ah, back to my treatise," he said in a drawn and exhausted voice. "Or maybe a visit down below to see what Holly Clarke is doing. She's always good for some action at midday." He made a gesture with his fist pounding into his palm. "At any time, really, not just at midday." He got up and scanned the room. "Could use a little wall art in here. Something to liven the place up a bit, Schefield. Kind of barren in here. I always think empty walls are depressing. They say it's a reflection of the inner mind. Oh well, have it your way. *Hasta luego!*"

12

After Lunz left I was spent and drained. He had cut the wind from my sails. What could I do? I swore not to close the door to my room. Sequester myself inside like a prisoner in solitary. I thought about the card that was left in Mona's book. The swastika. Who else could have done it but Lunz. The next time I see him I will push him for an explanation. I turned my attention to the open textbook in front of me but read barely a page before closing it. Perhaps this was a good time to take a break from my morning studies. Take a book to the library and find a quiet room and a desk and a chair and let the prisms of light through the stained-glass windows cleanse my soul of the toxins Lunz left me with. Or I could just stroll across campus—that always did me well. Sit and stare at my friends, the gargoyles. Or maybe see what Mona was up to. The sky was clear and phosphorescent and tiled with air from a warm yellow sun.

I left the dorm and walked to the quad and sat on a bench and leaned back and stretched my legs and watched thin vaporous clouds form and dissolve in the sky like smoke curling out of a billiard pipe. A buzz of students passed. I could almost feel the hustle-bustle of motion though my mind paid hardly more attention than it might to the blur of images that flash by the window of a city bus. My thoughts returned to Mona. I wondered if she was busy studying. I enjoyed being with her. She was one of those people who could always make you laugh. I realized I did not have her upbeat personality. How crazy it is that opposites attract: electrons and protons. Drawn together like some magnetic force of nature.

I was tempted to see if she was in her room but the thought of the unscripted visit from Lunz had left me with a feeling of inner gloom that I had yet to rid myself of. I felt unusually outwitted—the first such feeling in the short time I had been at Bradford. Could it be that I was homesick? This, however, I knew not to be the case given how grateful I was to have liberated my psyche from my father's solemn life during the years I spent in the house.

Flinging my backpack over my shoulder, I left campus and walked to Mulberry Street in Huntington Wells. I was not sure where I was destined but there was a welcome feeling of comfort in leaving campus. Down Mulberry for a block. I turned onto a narrow street with brick sidewalks and quaint shops and stopped and looked at the sky again for a second. Twenty yards on, I entered Salento Café. I had been there with Mona when we were discovering Bradford and its environs. It was a good café and I had fond memories of it. I wished Mona was here now.

I went inside and sat at a table. The room was humble and quiet and sparsely lit, salvaging most of its light from what came through the French doors and windows that faced the narrow street. Students gathered in gregarious groups. A young woman sat alone at a table hunched over a writing tablet, oblivious to everything around her—the music, the chatter, the laughter. I wanted to talk to her but I knew it would be rude. A version of how Lunz invaded my privacy almost daily. Perhaps I should text Mona. Perhaps she could come over. If she were to join me I knew I would feel better. But I didn't do it. I needed to cleanse myself of the venom Lunz spewed.

I bought a cup of coffee and thought about my classes. Was a major in government such a grand idea? I had no better option at the present, however. More people came into the café. Three groups now, talking and laughing. The girl continued to write as if deep in thought. A letter to a boyfriend? A girlfriend? A journal? A diary? I had kept a diary for a while in high school after reading a book by Anaïs Nin. I managed to keep it going for almost a year and then quit rather abruptly. Quit for no special reason. Months later, I went back and read the lissome words I had set on the pages—funny how much they revealed about me at that time. Perhaps I should start a diary again.

My thoughts came back to Lunz. Why is it we revisit an unpleasant moment of the day? I stared at the cup of dark coffee, dropped a sugar cube in, stirred it and took a sip. How many times had I vowed to run Lunz out of my room the second he showed at my door? How many times had I failed? Was I the only one Lunz was taunting? Why was I unable to stand up to him? Lunz, always playing the main character, the lead role. A sense of helplessness moved through me. Oddly though, there was something about Lunz that did not add up. I had no trouble believing he was a racist and probably a Nazi. And yet, he came across as an opportunist who was ready to float his boat in whatever direction the wind blew. What was the long game he was playing, and why was he trying to drag me along with him?

I took my phone from my pocket and again toyed with the

idea of texting Mona. *What if she is with another guy? Or busy studying? Or with a girlfriend?* I wished I had more confidence when it came to women. I wondered yet again if I was falling in love, was already in love. I laughed. Of course I was in love.

The ambiance of the café, the warm and comforting feeling, helped lift my mood and cleanse my thoughts of Lunz. I was happy I stopped in. I took a book from my backpack and began reading a novel from the list in English class. *The Great Gatsby.* Two books that were assigned for the next couple of weeks. *The Great Gatsby* and *Animal Farm.* I liked the books that were yet to come, some of which I had read in high school: *The Catcher in the Rye* and *A Confederacy of Dunces.*

Reading *The Catcher in the Rye,* I remembered how I imagined I was Holden Caulfield, who had traded in all responsibility for a foolish romp around New York City after he was kicked out of boarding school. *That's it, I'll be a writer,* I thought, suddenly convincing myself that this was my destiny. *A great and famous writer. I can live in Key West or Bimini or maybe even take up residence in Cuba as Hemingway had done. Dine on fresh fish I catch in the Gulf Stream and drink rum at La Floridita and other holes in Cuba, the haunts where Hemingway swilled many a drink.*

I had read all of Hemingway's books. Had even gone to the house in Oak Park not far from Hinsdale. Had stood in front of it. Though privately owned today, it remains a national monument.

Feeling better, I read a few pages of *The Great Gatsby* then set the book down. *Yes, indeed, I will be a writer of fiction,* I thought as I sat in the somber and soulful café. *Maybe I have been delivered this guy Lunz as a foil for my first book. Who knows…why not?* I was buoyed by the possibility. *Didn't Norman Mailer start writing when he was in college, having published his first short story while at Harvard?* The tide of despair Lunz had left me with was gradually dissipating like fog that spreads across Bradford in the early morning hours before it slips into thin mist and vanishes.

My phone pinged. A text from Mona. My heart was in my throat.

— Stopped by your room but you weren't there.

— I'm over at Salento Café on Mulberry Street.

— Everything OK?

— Yes, Fine.

— Can I join you?

— Yes, yes, please do!

— On my way. Ten minutes.

My mood shot high. I went to the men's room and looked in the mirror and shoved hair this way and that and groaned and returned to the table.

Barely ten minutes and Monique came bounding into the café. Sitting at the table, she said, "Couldn't do any more book work. I'm caught up on everything. But you know how I am. I have to go over all my assignments again and again. Oh well, that's just how I am, I guess. I think I inherited it from my father. He's such a thorough person. One of those lawyers who wants everything to be perfect. All the i's dotted and t's crossed as he used to say." She laughed bright and happy.

I explained that I was heading to the library to do some work. I laughed and said, "But my feet took me to the café. I read a little of *The Great Gatsby*. I swear, Fitzgerald is a spectacular writer. This Gatsby fellow he writes about is a pretty shallow person. It's amazing how well Fitzgerald describes him."

"Well…hope I don't ruin your day but I suppose I should

mention that I saw Krause Lunz this afternoon," Mona said. "He was wandering around the hall by my room. He didn't notice me. As soon as I saw him I slipped into my room. I think he was looking for Holly Clarke. He kept banging on her door. He seemed to think she was in her room and that she was avoiding him. That's the feeling I got. He knocked for quite a while, harder and harder. I knew Holly was not there. She told me she was going to study with some friends. I don't know what Lunz's problem is. Even if she was in her room, it should have been clear she didn't want to be bothered. I think he eventually figured she was not there. I heard her door open very slowly. It's easy to tell it from my room. I'm pretty certain he went inside. A little while after that I heard the door close. I cracked my door and looked to see if he was there but he had left."

I told Mona that Lunz is barging into my room almost everyday and that the stuff he's saying is getting real screwy, and that I think he actually believes it. He says he's getting most of it from the internet and social media. "He keeps pushing me to read it," I said. "From what I can tell the sites are super radical, loaded with conspiracies of all kinds. I don't know what's going on with the guy but he seems to be…remember when we learned in psychology about how people can become psychotic, especially if some unresolved issue is burning inside them? The more he says, the more he seems to be slipping off the rails, almost as if he's about to crack."

We stayed at the café for hours, putting all thoughts of Lunz far behind us. Later we went to the cafeteria for dinner and then to Mona's room and found ourselves in bed. With the sweetest eyes, she whispered, "Ah, *mon amour, mon amour, mon amour.*"

My heart trembled.

13

Morning arrived. The view of the campus from Mona's window gave forth a cloudy drizzly forenoon. A misty London kind of day that held a hazy sun in a pale-yellow shadow of a gray sky. Fog dotted the quadrangle like fluffy cushions and hid the tops of the old buildings and made students little more than mechanical robots moving randomly along on their way to class.

By eleven o'clock I was in my room, thoughts of Mona still with me. It was the first time I had been in love, had ever experienced deep and urgent feelings for someone. I thought about the curious way the world works. There I was, a student at Bradford, and there in the same dorm was someone I adored. What were the odds of that, I wondered. Is there some type of celestial alignment that brings people together at just the right moment? It really mattered not at all how it is that two out of eight billion people on the planet find each other. It happened and that was what I rejoiced in.

Lying on the bed, I sensed the presence of someone standing outside my door. "Krause Wilhelm Lunz," I uttered.

"Slick! How did you know?"

"Call it vibes."

"Good ones or bad ones?"

"I will soon know." Swinging my feet over the edge of the bed I stared at the wall then got up and shuffled to the window in a way that declared I had more important matters to be occupied with than to pulverize an hour with Lunz.

"A lovely day out there, wouldn't you say? You'd think we've been transformed to Oxford College in jolly old England? Could be fooled into believing it. The buildings, the mist, the fog."

"I suppose."

"Well, I had a glorious night. Spent it with horny Holly."

"Last time you were here you said you and Holly were finished…kaput, as I recall."

"Oh…really?"

"Memory slipping? There's medicine for that, isn't there?"

"Funny guy."

I wondered if Lunz had fabricated his claim of a night with Holly given what Mona said about how he had been lurking around her room but hadn't connected with her. More and more I was beginning to believe he was manufacturing much of what he told me about his life. But what did I care if his endless tales about him and Holly Clarke were fact or fiction? Mere splashes of paint on a canvas. I was getting plenty sick of hearing about it. I turned away from the window.

"Gotta get to lecture. Don't you ever go to class?"

Some. Already told you I'm a freaking genius."

"No humblebrag from this guy."

"It's true. What can I say. Children of shrinks are known to be the smartest kids. And, of course, I got a double dose of it…homozygous dominant in genetic parlance."

"So, you don't go to class."

"Now and then, now and then. So what?"

"How do you keep a GPA going with that?"

"Perfect 4.0," he blurted, suggesting he did not like the challenge. "Fuck the classes. My singular goal now is to finish my treatise. It's taking up most of my time. It's freakin' spectacular. I'm thinking of publishing it."

"This group you keep referring to. Does it have a name?"

"Of course it does. The National Peoples Party. The NPP. There!"

"Thought you were pushing fascism? Sounds like pablum to me. Peoples Party? Not very crusty sounding."

"Good god, Schefield, you don't put fascism in the title of your party. You don't call it the National Fascist Party. For Christ's sake, any sane idiot would know not to do that. All I care about now is finishing up my treatise. Damn near done. You can be one of the first to read it."

"National Peoples Party, sort of like Q-Anon, I suppose. Q-Anon and all those others. The Oath Keepers. The Three Percenters. Is that it?"

"The problem with those groups is that they never really knew what they believed. Okay, they had some good ideas, a few. But they never pulled them together. Couldn't keep from tripping over their own dicks. Just a bunch of radical right-wing frat boys pushing radical right-wing philosophies to a minuscule pack of pissed-off followers. You don't have to be Aristotle to know that formula will get you nowhere. We know exactly how to do it; we're organized. Real tight. Not a bunch of cheese heads like in those groups. The NPP is packed with smart people. If you don't have that, you won't make it out of the gate. Mark my word, the people in this country will line up behind the NPP like they did in 1933 in Krautland. Back then the Nazis were officially called the National Socialist German Workers' Party. Just wait, history *does* repeat itself. We're getting ready to run our first candidate for Congress. It's all planned out. Right down to the last grit. A nice deep-red congressional district in rural Alabama. Way out in the sticks. Can't lose. Sprawling district full of rednecks. Nothing but purebred rednecks and hayseeds. The kind of place where people are sick of what's going on in the country. We'll have no trouble winning. All but guaranteed. Soon as people hear what we stand for they'll come running to vote for our guy." He looked at his watch but kept talking. "That's just the beginning. To make it all work, we'll need to get the perfect person for top dog, for prez…someone who can keep everyone pumped and the wheels greased. That's goddamn important. Get the right person elected prez and the rest of the dominos will fall down. Tic, tic, tic, one after another."

"Pretty tall order."

"In the history of the world there have always been fascists ready to step in and take the reins. Someone who knows what to do and how to do it, how to consolidate power. Someone who operates from a position of fear. The fact remains, all people are just little children. It's far easier to float along than to try to right the boat. It takes guts to do that…takes fortitude. Every fascist leader knew there is a short supply of that in the world. People are basically cowards. You could summarize what happened in Germany in one sentence: I didn't do anything when they came for the others, and the others didn't do anything when they came for me. When we get control, the whole damn Constitution goes out the window. Yes, freedom of speech, too. What is freedom of speech? Nothing but a way to carp about what you don't like. Carp, carp, carp, but nothing ever changes. It's like those parents who let their kids do whatever the hell they want. I heard about it all my life from my mother, Shrink 1, the one who tries to unwind screwed up kids. I heard about how those bratty little bastards get whatever they want and how it balls up their whole life. That's what freedom of speech does! In a good fascist society, there's no need for that shit. The government will do all the thinking. Total liberation for the masses. When we finally get our man in Casa Blanca the rest will be easy. Just take the government apart piece by piece."

"Get rid of the Constitution and what do you do for laws?"

"Cut it out! Laws are a joke. What were Hitler's laws? Mussolini's laws?"

"Sounds like fucking chaos."

"Chaos is when people are drugged into thinking they're being governed by laws."

"You know, Lunz, I used to think that you come in here and fling bullshit around just to see where it will stick. That it's all some kind of game. But it's not a game, is it? You really believe this shit."

A faint smile crossed Lunz's face for a moment, then vanished.

"I've got to go," I said, picking up a book.

"Christ, you'd think this was an institution of higher education, or something," Lunz said.

I stuffed the book into my backpack, escorted Lunz to the door, returned to my desk, and flipped open the notebook with the beginnings of my novel. It was a ragged and flimsy start. I knew little about what the story would entail. Something that had to do with Bradford. It was the best I could do at present. I read what I had recently written. Should I make Lunz the evil and flawed person he came across as? Or someone with human imperfections like the rest of us? Or should he be a real bastard? I knew that ordinary people, flawed or not, are complex beasts. I put my pen down and thought about Krause Lunz. Perhaps his actions merely belied evilness. There was something about this strange loaf Krause Lunz that never quite makes sense.

This was not going to be easy. The more I read what I had written, the less I liked it. The character fashioned after Lunz was hardly more than a cardboard cutout. A flimsy, crappy cardboard cutout. No flesh, no bones. No blood, grist, or marrow. I wondered if all the great writers felt that way about their work. Orhan Pamuk, Stephen King. Dean Koontz, Toni Morrison, Patrick Modiano. I especially liked Modiano's writing, the way the words blended so perfectly, so smoothly. How they seemed to float off the page like delicate literary dragonflies. I snapped the notebook closed and raced to biology class.

14

I did not see Krause Lunz for over a week though I knew my luck would not persist. From my desk I heard footsteps thumping down the hall. I grimaced and waited for Lunz to appear.

"Ha, still here," Lunz said, inviting himself in. "Thought you may have fled from Brad...fled and taken sweetie pie with you."

Before I could utter a word, Lunz was halfway in the room carrying a thick, bound document. He held it six inches over my desk and let it fall with a sonorous thud. Blazen on the front was a red cover with a white circle in which the letters NPP were inscribed in black letters. The whole affair bore a troublingly resemblance to the swastika design used by the Nazis. Across the top in gothic letters were the words *Unser Kampf*. Along the bottom: A Manifesto on America by Krause Wilhelm Lunz.

"There you have it. All the vast and sundry problems that are pulling America down spelled out in words that even the Neanderthals in some Appalachian holler will understand. Sixty-five thousand words, all two hundred and ten pages of sheer genius. Pure enlightenment! When the gumps, palookas, and thimble heads of America read it they'll pop right out of their fucking skin."

I glanced at the document as though it were a slab of plutonium.

"Go ahead. Go ahead. Take a look, take a look. She ain't gonna bite you. Go ahead." He watched my reaction. "I see your knowledge of German leaves much to be desired. Let me translate. *Unser Kampf*...Our Struggle. Sounds sort of familiar, huh? Good ole' Hit published his version as *Mein Kampf*...My Struggle. It came out in 1925. Huge best seller. Well, no, not at first. True, it took a while for it to catch on. But when it did it surpassed the Bible in sales in Krautland. It got his whole movement rolling like water tumbling over a dam. It opened the eyes of the German people to all the troubles they were having; they became instant believers. They fell in line like a bunch of ducklings." Lunz waved a hand at the raft of paper on my desk. "Herr Hitler pulled it off perfectly with *Mein Kampf*. He laid out the problems in a way that any Kraut could understand. He knew what was wrong with the country and how to fix it. That much he knew. That much the mustachioed gremlin knew. And when he got up and screeched his rants and threw his fist at the Germans and roared about how he would fix everything, they were nothing but little puppies. All he had to do was tell them what they wanted to hear. Find out what the problems were and tell them he had the solutions."

"You think I'm going to waste my time with this shit, Lunz?"

"Just shows you don't get it."

"I haven't read it. Probably won't, in fact."

"You will. The curious mind cannot ignore suspense."

"Don't be so sure."

"And now I'm planning to get the whole brilliant piece published. A fellow in our squad knows someone who will do it. Ever heard of Otto Barringer?

"Can't say I have."

"The guy is a whiz when it comes to getting things done. Straight out of Krautland. His parents shoveled him over here to the Brad to get a dose of how things are done on this side of the pond. He's become a kingpin in the NPP. Has loads of great ideas. Sort of our Hermann Goering, you might say. Otto read it and thinks it'll be a massive best seller."

"Now you're *really* hallucinating. Need to lay off the mushrooms."

"You'll see, just wait. Once you've read it, you'll be convinced...nickel ninety-eight says you'll even want to join the NPP. I'm reckoning you might even be one of our first converts we flip here at the Brad." When he realized nothing more was coming from me, he stuffed his hands in his pockets. "Big busy day, gotta go."

"You can take this pile of tripe with you on the way out," I said, sliding it across my desk as though it were sprinkled with Zika virus. "Unless you don't mind it ending up as a door stop here in my room, that is."

"Ah, ha, ha, ha," Lunz chortled, as he slipped out the door.

Sure enough, barely a few minutes after Lunz left I began paging through the tome on my desk, flipping to a page here and there. It was chock-full of all the wild and desultory whims I expected from Lunz.

> My name is Krause Wilhelm Lunz. Here, you will learn about the National Peoples Party, the NPP, and you will learn how it will transform America into a better place. Much time has gone into the planning

of the NPP. Much historical justification underlies its origins. You will see that two simple and basic concepts, just two, are the foundations for the NPP. First, America was always intended to be a country of white people. Second, America is a Christian country. We at the NPP did not make it this way. Its origins date to the moment the first settlers set foot on the soil of what today is America.

I came to these realizations after my own personal struggle, attempting to rectify the nature of how the great country called America had failed in its goals. Goals that are not difficult to understand. Goals that every American of a certain type and disposition will come to agree with because these are fundamental to the core strategies of how the problems of America can be eliminated.

We at NPP are not racists. We are not the Ku Klux Klan. We do not hate people who are not like us, though we shall surely be accused of such. Rather, we are here to lead America back to the very roots upon which it was founded so it can move forward with purpose, with a fabric to live proudly by, with goals for the future, with justification for the beliefs that form the true heart of the American lifestyle.

This country claims to have been founded on grand and lofty beliefs and attitudes. Today we hear perpetually about the great experiment that is American democracy, how it is in deep peril today. Yet, if you think for a moment, you will realize that democracy never existed in this country, not now, not ever. It is and has been a grand and harsh myth to keep people in line, that and nothing more. The power of the masses can be overwhelming when the conditions are right. Or that power can be turned over to greedy and self-serving politicians. Politicians who care little about what is good for the people they are supposed to be serving. Fish always rot from the head down. It is up to the people of this country to scrub out the rot that is controlling their lives, that is draining their lifeblood. In this manifesto, I will lay out in perfect and clear words how the people of America can take back the country before it is too late.

Can America become what it was meant to be? Read and decide.

Can Americans take control of their own destiny? Read and decide.

Just like you, I once believed that America is a good country with the interests of the people at heart. Yes, I too believed that. It is the line, the orthodox, we are all taught. The schools, the churches, all of them teach this. And so, from our earliest days we begin to believe this. Never questioning it, we accept every part of it. But America has tricked its people for centuries. Good people have been kept down. Anyone who disagrees is marginalized, pushed to the side. And then one day, I began to see everything very clearly. I saw what a hoax America is. I saw how it panders to the weakest. How it wants everyone to be the same. I, too, had been tricked. I, too, believed that every politician—the good ones and yes even the bad ones—were in it for us. Isn't that why we sent them to Washington, to do good for the country? And yet they are barely there a day before they have sold their soul to any Shylock who will toss them a nickel.

When I realized that, it became clear that the time had come for change because you, me, everyone who looks like us are the true victims of slavery. Do not be fooled or tricked into believing otherwise. The struggle for America today, Our Struggle as laid out here in *Unser Kampf* is to see beneath the whitewash. To look at who will save this country. When you are done reading this, I am convinced you will join the NPP. We can control our own destiny. We do not need greedy politicians to make promises that they know they will never keep. Look into your own lives and ask, is the government working for me? Or am I working for the government? We are nothing but cannon fodder. Used by politicians for their own glory. In *Unser Kampf* I will spell out every problem that Americans face. Most importantly, I will tell you in simple terms what can be done to save America before it is too late.

I could tell that I would find little good in the thousands of words in front of me. Paging through the manuscript, my fingers landed on a chapter titled, THE SOLUTION. Laid out in great detail was a plan for how the NPP would cleanse the country. How they would purify it. The more I read, the more disgusted I became. Oddly, a part of me was surprised at how carefully Lunz had avoided mentioning individual groups and specific people in his descriptions of the cleansing process. No mention of skin color—black, brown, or any other. Only slight mention of ethnic origin. It was all there, however, safely treasured away in words carefully selected so as not to reveal target populations, carefully worded like the opening fulminations of a Fox News monologue. *Yeah, how well this bastard Lunz performed his magic of hatred*, I thought. The vitriol of each page was laid out for readily accessible deniability when attacked by the droves of critics who would surely come at him. Most important, it was perfectly scribed to reach the dweebs, yokels, bumpkins, gumps, clodhoppers, dolts, and hillbillies, as Krause Lunz so lovingly called them. The people Lunz wanted above all to reach. I recalled the many times Lunz said that fascism comes from the people. It is the people—the citizens, yes, the dweebs, yokels, bumpkins, gumps, clodhoppers, dolts, and hillbillies—who would deliver the country to a fascist messiah when he (and surely it would be a man) finally comes to lead them out of their grief and hopelessness. They were the people the NPP needed to reach. Fascism is a cancer that grows from inside the beast. Slowly at first, like all cancers, until it has begun to consume the organism that is feeding it.

The solutions Lunz extolled were sleek and tightly hidden. First, only people who came to America of their own volition could qualify as citizens no matter what methods had tricked them into believing they had a right to be here. Being a citizen was no qualification, no justification, for residence in America. *I suppose that pretty much takes care of someone like Mona,* I thought. *People like her and probably twenty percent of the population of the country made up of African Americans, Hispanics, Latinos and Asians. After all, the Nazis exterminated millions of their own, not just Jews. Catholics, Gypsies, the homeless, and scores of others, citizens or not.*

Each page reflected the core of Lunz's beliefs. Now I knew there was little doubt that what Lunz pummeled me with almost daily came from deep inside him. How naïve of me to think otherwise. Now, I realized my father was right when he warned me about believing everyone was basically good.

I walked to the window and stared at the campus that was Bradford University—calm and kind. At the gargoyles atop the buildings across from me. The soft afternoon sun spread quiet harmony, bringing a pale blue glow to the granite buildings and the fading green grass of autumn. In the distance was the library. The twin complementing copper cupolas held a stately sheen. *If Lunz were to publish* Unser Kampf, *would it someday end up on a shelf there in the library,* I wondered. *Thereby soiling the words of the great writers of fiction, the deep thinkers of antiquity?* I felt my stomach knot up. I pulled the sash up in the hope of cleansing the room of the feeling of desperation Lunz's words had left me with. *What should I do with it? Burn it would be a good choice. Do people at universities, at places of higher education, places of enlightenment, have the right to produce such putrid?* I knew the answer. The First Amendment guarantees it. For a moment, I hated the First Amendment. *Just look at the hostile invectives that come from the podium in Congress almost daily. Where has the country gone wrong? Where…how?* It was getting worse all the time; I could not deny that. Every day, words and actions of governors targeted immigrants in places like Texas and Florida. Actions that fit perfectly with the diabolical menu Krause Wilhelm Lunz offered, a menu planned to grease the minds of Americans who believed they were getting shafted by people who were leaving behind all but that which they could carry and coming to this country out of mortal desperation. *Unser Kampf* had hit that target dead-on.

I thought about Mona. I could not possibly let her know what Lunz had given me. I prayed he would not deliver copies of his irreverent treatise to her and Holly Clarke and Jennifer Rubinstein and others in the dorm. How devastating it would be if she saw it. I knew that Mona throughout her life had been victim to the bile puked from the mouths of some people. Thinking of that brought a sense of deep and woeful sadness to me. And Jenifer Rubinstein? Surely, she had received her own tailored dose of antisemitic remarks over the years. How could she not? *But why would Krause Lunz wish to torment them more? Is that ultimately what he is really after…a desire to see how much mental anguish a person can take before striking back? Striking back or falling into tears. Is Lunz the schoolyard bully who pushes the smaller kids, the weaker kids, onto the ground again and again until they no longer get up? Until they looked up at him from the ground with eyes that say, 'I give up…please, let me alone'. The kindergarten bully who goes through the room knocking over the building blocks of the other kids? Is that Krause Lunz?*

I was filled with gloom of a kind I had not experienced since coming to Bradford.

15

A knock at the door. I knew from the gentle tapping that it was Mona. I quickly stowed *Unser Kamp* in the drawer. Opening the door, Mona stood like an apparition of wonderous delight. Eyes aglow as always. A smile shared the inner warmth that was the essence of her inner spirit. I gave her a big hug and a passionate kiss.

"You can do *that* again," she said in the jolliest way. She came in and sat on the bed. "I had so much to study today I thought I'd never get it all done. But I'm caught up now. Are you hungry?"

We crossed campus hand in hand. The midday sun was eclipsed by a thin layer of clouds as if shining through sheets of Belgian lace. We bought sandwiches and chips and soda at the cafeteria and sat at a quiet table on the edge of the room and talked about our classes and tests and homework. Mona said, "The good news is that Krause Lunz is finally leaving me alone...I think so. He hasn't come by in...in, I don't know...a week, probably. Maybe two. So, now I leave my door open a little, though one time I'm pretty certain I heard him going over to Holly Clarke's room. I'm not sure, but you can usually tell from the heavy boots he wears and the way he knocks on the door. Pounding as if demanding she open it."

I wondered if I should tell Mona about my visit from Lunz but decided against it. I wished Krause Lunz was gone. Gone not just from Bradford but gone from the planet. Gone forever. And take with him his profane vituperation.

"Well, I heard that Lunz might be getting ready to leave Bradford. That's what I heard," Mona said. "Oh, I hope so. I only mention it because of how good it would make me feel. I still get nervous knowing he's lurking around the dorm. In fact, I think he was in my room again. I'm not totally sure but I think so."

I ran my fingers through my hair and looked at the ceiling. "I don't understand. I thought you said he hasn't been by in a while."

"That's right. I haven't seen him, is what I mean. And I usually lock the door to my room whenever I go out…."

"I don't get it."

"You see, Holly Clarke told me Lunz has a master key to all the rooms, just like the one the dorm monitor has. They give it to the monitor in case he needs to get in a room. In case someone is hurt or something. Of course, the dorm monitors are appointed by the school. As far as I know they're vetted before the school appoints them. But apparently not vetted so well. Holly said Lunz told her the dorm monitor is a friend of his. In fact, he belongs to that group, the weird society Lunz is part of. Apparently, there are quite a few people here on campus who are part of it. You never hear much about them, though."

"I met the dorm monitor. He's a guy named Howie Berman. He came by my room a while ago and introduced himself. I brought up our problems with Lunz. He said there was not much he could do. Didn't say he was friends with Lunz, though."

"Well, it's not just my room. According to Holly, Lunz has been in other rooms. The story is that Berman gave Lunz the master key and he made a copy. He can go anywhere he wants. Jennifer Rubinstein knows Howie Berman pretty well. She said he comes around and bugs her to go to the Jewish Community Center. She never goes."

"I'm surprised Lunz has any Jewish friends," I said.

"Holly Clarke said Lunz told her he wants to know what people in the dorm are up to…he keeps track of lots of people. He said the FBI is watching his group and he's ticked off about it and he's determined to find out who the perps at Bradford are. That's why he's snooping around, going in and out of the rooms when students are out. Now I'm really worried. Yeah, I know I just told you Lunz is finally leaving me alone and that he doesn't come to my room and bother me when I'm there. He stopped doing that. But I'm beginning to feel like he's stalking me the way he does to Holly sometimes. I don't know, that's how I feel."

My thoughts flashed to Lunz's paranoid rants about the FBI and how they had moles on campus who were tagging him and the other NPP members.

Mona said, "Holly told me Lunz has been talking about fascism and how the country is in a bad place right now and it needs to be fixed very, very soon. She said that she tried to cut him off…tried to stop seeing him because when he gets going he becomes almost insane, he keeps getting worse. He's impossible to stop. And he keeps telling Holly that she's crazy for having a Jew girl as a roommate, his words for Jennifer. I'm really worried he's going to do something crazy. He's becoming more insane all the time."

"There's nothing we can do. We can't change the locks, the school wouldn't let us."

We considered bringing the issue to the attention of the school. But how could we do it? What would we say? Tell them we think one of the students has a key to the dorm rooms and that he's been poking around in everyone's stuff? Say that? And, the fact is, Mona had no hard evidence of it except for what she heard from a friend. The school would then have to talk to Holly Clarke and Jennifer Rubinstein and maybe even to Howie Berman, and probably Lunz himself. It would become a great big ugly mess and neither of us wanted that.

"My mother always used to say, 'Mona, don't make waves. It's not worth it. If you do, you will find that people will not believe you the way they would a white person'. She said she did that a few times when she was a young girl and it did not go well so she never did it again. She said you need to have a certain type of privilege to be a whistleblower in this country."

"Now what? We can't let Krause Lunz just wander in and out of our rooms."

Mona said, "On top of it, Holly thinks Lunz has been rifling through her dresser when she's out. Jennifer Rubinstein told Holly the same thing. If it wasn't Lunz, then maybe Berman. They said some of their intimate things were gone. That much they're sure of."

"I've talked with Lunz a lot. I can assure you, not by choice. He comes to my room a couple times a week and pontificates about all kinds of paranoid stuff. I wonder if his psychiatrist parents know how crazy he is? He mostly raves about the government, says it's out of control. That the Deep State has developed ways to shadow everyone. That it's made up of hard-core government stooges who will do anything they're told. That's what he says. Zombie-like people who are being controlled with huge amounts of drugs. He's exhausting to listen to. You know me…I have no capacity to send people away. Something that came from my father, I guess…I don't know. He's a very patient man. Hardly ever loses his temper. Mostly what Lunz talks about now is fascism. He thinks it's the solution for all the troubles in America."

"For people like me and Jennifer Rubinstein. I know that's what he means," Mona said.

"He's got this big manuscript describing his beliefs—how fascism will solve everything. His manifesto, as he calls it. He left a copy with me just this morning. Said it holds the foundation of the beliefs of that NPP group of his. Said they will take over the country, that it's going to be a big struggle to do it but in the end they'll succeed."

"Maybe we should ask the school to reassign us to a different building," Mona said. "That might be a solution."

"I don't know, possibly. But what if Lunz has connections all over campus? Other people like Howie Berman perhaps. Lunz seems to know a hell of a lot of people. He could have a keyring full of master keys for all we know. I say we wait. Maybe he'll leave us alone. There's nothing he wants from us."

16

I took the writing tablet that had the beginning of my novel
from the desk drawer and added several paragraphs. It was
starting to take shape. The character patterned after Lunz
had the elements of a real person. I had no trouble granting him
a dark side—that came easy. But trying to fill in assorted patches
of humanity with a few milligrams of kindness was far more difficult. I tried, nonetheless. I knew I had to make the character
complete lest it be someone who was purely diabolical and nothing more. Fitzgerald had achieved his near-perfect portrayal of
Jay Gatsby despite the tragic elements embodied in the man.
What a feat!

I shaped the story after my short time at Bradford: Mona
and myself and Holly Clarke and Jennifer Rubinstein. But ultimately it was about Krause Lunz—a young firebrand who came
to Bradford with plans to salvage what little good he believed was
left in America. All were present on the pages, delicately masked
of their true selves.

With each sentence I was certain that my future lies in writing. I no longer had an interest in a job in government or the
diplomatic core. It still seemed like a worthy profession. I

remembered with fondness listening to my father's friend, the ambassador, as he talked with gusto about his long career in the State Department. The countries where he worked. The many heads of state he had come to know, some good, some vile. But the more I pondered a life of embassy work, the drearier it seemed. What if I were stuck in…in who knows where…in Zimbabwe? Would I like it or hate it? Would the work be challenging or strictly repetitious? Something to be enjoyed or something to be despised? True, I knew I had a capacity to tolerate the great hash of humanity that walks this planet, or so I believed. But even in that, I found myself tested when in the presence of Krause Lunz. Yes, maybe the life of a novelist was my destiny—the sort of lofty goal college students aspire to regardless of any real potential of success. I fantasized about a life of pen and ink. I will find a simple little bungalow on some simple little island in the Caribbean. Or perhaps it will be a small flat in the French Quarter in New Orleans where I'll peck out the words of my fiction like Truman Capote or Tennessee Williams. How will I survive while hoping to be discovered? Who knows. Wait tables, perhaps. Each day I continued diligently to add words to my novel.

A knock on the door. The unmistakable *rat-tat-tat* of Krause Lunz. Now, each person—Mona, Lunz, one or two others—had their own signature way of setting a knuckle to the door. I shut the notebook, slipped it in the drawer, and closed it tightly. With not so much as a second tap Lunz swung the door open and shambled into the room, shoulders loose, hands in his pockets. Hair mussed and flattened onto his forehead suggesting a hard night with Bacchus.

"You look damn fucking chopped, Lunz. How about you drag your shabby ass on down the hall."

Lunz steered himself in the direction of the window. "Busted up last night with my tribe, that's all. Partied like hell-fire," he mumbled, in a raspy voice while he viewed the campus hanging onto the windowsill as if it were the rail of a rolling steam ship. "Don't you ever pachanga?" He glanced over his shoulder for my reaction. "Nah, probably not. You don't look like the partying kind." Returning to the window again, he said, "You might not know it but Bradford is one hell of a good place to hold a rager. We do it all the time. You'll learn…once you're here a while. I mean like what the hell kind of person comes to a place like this to study…as if it's some kind of pedagogical institution or something. As if you might actually learn something here…seriously? If you're going to spend four goddam years here, for Christ's sake go out and get a load on now and then, Schefield."

"Well, I didn't come here to party," I informed Lunz.

"Meh! We had a real good blowout, oh yeah. Bashed all night. A bunch of us from the NPP over at a guy's place off campus…the doghouse, we call it. And from what I heard last night everything is moving along just fine with the group. Smooth as silk." He tramped his way to the chair and squashed himself down and dragged his feet onto the ottoman and closed his eyes for a moment. "By the way. Saw your honey, Monique, this afternoon walking across campus." When he realized I wasn't going to reply, he said, "Well…I didn't stop by to talk about chicks. Hell, I could waste the whole afternoon talking about Holly Clarke. No matter what, she's definitely hot, let me tell you. And Rubinstein, I've been wondering about Rubinstein. Like I said, I'm not proud—"

"Lunz, do you have something meaningful to say, because you may not believe it but I do have a lot of schoolwork. Not like you, apparently. I still can't figure out how you manage to—"

"Okay, okay, okay, let's not go there. What about *Unser Kampf?*"

"What about it?

"Well?"

"Barely read any of it if you need to know. But what I can tell from the little I did read is that it's filled with a lot of slippery goddamn conspiracies. Pure horse shit. Nobody's going to believe that crap."

"And that alone, Mr. Schefield, shows what little you know."

"It's teeming with conspiracies. You pretty much covered every fucking one of them. Be honest, Lunz, you don't believe the crap in that pile of rubbish you wrote."

Lunz slipped down against the back of the chair for a second then lifted himself up and moved his head from side to side and rubbed his neck.

"I figured out what you're doing. I'm your test case. You want to see how I'll react to your morbid creation. If it flops here it might flop everywhere."

"You haven't read it. How would you know?" Lunz mumbled. "And besides, it's been fully catechized by others. And furthermore, it's not intended for people like you, a classic nerd who overthinks everything. It's for the clowns who don't have any wits at all. Those are the beefsteaks the NPP needs to reach. Admit it, Schefield, this country is filled with a raft of assholes dumb as fence posts. Barely half of the eligible voting population casts a ballot. Know why? Because they can't trouble themselves to find out which candidate will work on their behalf. That's why! Too busy watching *Dancing with the Stars* on the idiot box. They want to be told who to vote for. But most importantly, they want a savior to bring them out of the darkness and into the Holy Land. *Unser Kampf* will do that. It will be their Bible. They'll learn how wonderful fascism is and how it is the *only* solution for everything that ails them."

"The final solution?"

Lunz continued unfazed. "They'll see how important it is that they are protected and cared for."

"The final solution?" I repeated.

"Your words, not mine! *Unser Kampf:* Our Struggle. Not My Struggle as Czar Hitler put it. This struggle has been going on since the day the country was formed. That much the people of America will realize." Lunz leaned back and yawned wide.

"Spare me your babble."

"Ah…maybe. Anyway, in a few weeks a bunch of us from the NPP will be going down to Bama to help with the campaign of Horace Crockett, the hick who's running on the NPP ticket. I told you about him. He's going to win by a landslide. He's running against a Democrat and a Republican. Neither of them stand a fucking chance. In fact, the polls show Crockett with a huge lead, almost twenty points. You haven't heard about it in the news because they're trying to pretend it's not happening. They've got their heads in the sand like the proverbial ostrich. As if, if they don't report on it, Crockett will lose. Shows what a bunch of dimwits the media are."

"I read about the guy in the *Times*. You may not believe it, but even being the nerd that I am, as you say, I do follow what's going on in the world. They have a copy of the *Times* in the library."

"Glory be! You read it in the fucking *New York Times*, no less."

"Try reading it. You need a better-grounded information base than the crock you get on the internet."

"I sure as hell am not going to read the drivel that comes from the *Times*. That's for sure."

"Afraid you might learn something?"

"Hell no. My parents always had the *Times* delivered to the house. I used to read it until I realized it was pure left-wing propaganda, nothing but food for the masses. Worse than religion."

"They've run a few stories about this Crockett guy in Alabama. Talked about his freakish attitudes."

"Doesn't matter what you, or the *Times*, or what anyone else thinks, Crockett is a shoo-in to be elected. He'll be the first NPP member in Congress."

"So you get *one* person in Congress…one damn person. BFD, Lunz."

"*It is a BFD*. You know, Schefield, sometimes you're fucking impossible to talk to. "You can be a real dork when you want to be."

"Did those parents of yours, the two shrinks, did they teach you it's all right to insult people?"

"My parents didn't teach me shit! Everything I learned, I learned on my own. That's why universities, places like the Brad, are so useless. People come here with a brain and walk out as eidolons." He could tell the word did not register with me. "Look it up. Pull out your Webster and get a definition."

"It was perfectly obvious what you meant."

"God, I'm tired."

"Already said you look like shit."

"Not tired that way. Tired of having to educate people like you. But you're not the only one. I'm doing this all the time now, it seems. Gets to wearing thin. Therein lies our real struggle, our true *Unser Kampf.* Getting our message out will be the ultimate big struggle. I'm not delusional. We just need to get the right people doing NPP promos for us. The right kind of Pols. The ones that people will listen to. See, that's why the folks in the backwoods of Bama love Horace Crockett. He speaks to them. Just straight talk. Not like the dumbass Democrats who insult people and then think they're going to vote for them."

"Maybe. Who knows?"

"Jesus Christ, you might be starting to catch on, Schefield. Might be hope for you yet." Lunz sat up and stretched. "Man, my back is sore as hell…wow. Must have been from hosing Holly Clarke half the night. She's good but it's like going to the gym."

"Thought you lit up with your NPP jocks?"

"I did…Later on, I did." He leaned forward and rubbed his back. "But you know, I've been wondering if I can get Holly to line up a threesome, a *ménage à trois.* Me, her, Rubinstein."

Bizarre comment, I thought, given Lunz's malignant attitudes about Jews, until I realized that it was nothing more than a carnal instinct on his part.

"Anyway, when Crockett gets elected down in Bama the left-wing cabal at *The New York Times* will sit up real fast. All the people at the pinko cable news stations, too. You'll hear all the dykes and bitches on MSNBC and CNN whimpering to beat hell, probably wet their tighty-whities right there on camera. It'll be a goddamn eureka moment. A real goddamn eureka moment! I can hear it now. They'll all pretend like they didn't see it coming. Like they got sucker-punched or something. They're good at that. Always pretending they got tricked when they get the story wrong, as if someone fed them bullshit information. They have to come up with some flim-flam excuse to keep from losing their twenty-million-dollar contracts. I'm planning to get Crockett to come here to the Brad to talk to the students. I'm sure I can arrange a meet-and-greet for you." Lunz yawned as if gasping for air.

"I heard you have a key to the dorm rooms."

He glanced instinctively at the ceiling. "Who told you that?"

"Well?"

"Well, what?"

"Do you have a master key?"

"What the hell would I do with dorm room keys?"

"Heard you got the key from Howie Berman. Know who Berman is?"

"Yeah, yeah, I know Berman. So what? Daddy's filthy rich. Big hedge-fund guy or something. Lots of houses everywhere."

"He told me he's from Brooklyn."

"I don't know. Maybe. But they've got a joint on Long Island. And a shack on the Upper East Side. And a place in Florida, of course…it's practically a requirement, in Miami or Lauderdale. Not sure which. And a two-million-dollar hole out west somewhere…Taos, I think. Rich as hell like all the others like him at Brad. Crazy thing is, I tolerate Berman." Ever notice how funny some Jews are? Case in point, Seinfeld. Lots of others, too. Rodney Dangerfield, Mort Sahl, the comedians going way back."

"I heard Berman is a member of the NPP? Little surprised you'd let him into your group."

"You probably don't know it but there were plenty of Jewish Nazis in Germany. Go check out Helmuth Wilberg, a famous general in the Luftwaffe. And there were lots more in the Wehrmacht and the Kriegsmarine. Lots of them found their way into the SS. The reason is simple, people hate their own kind. Don't think so? Just look at India. The Brahmins dump on the classes below them and they all dump on the Shudras. Same old thing that's been going on for millennia. Same thing in Krautland when ole' Adolph was running things. Best place for a Jew to hide back then was in the SS. Betcha Tangsley never mentions *that* in his lectures, does he? Nah, he's totally sanitized what he tells you guys. This may not surprise you but when I took—ahem, when I *had* to take his class—we got into a big bruhaha right there in the classroom, me and Tangsley. It went on for ten minutes. Wow, was he ever pissed! You could tell no one had ever challenged him. Never! He was so pissed he started shaking. That cheap toup he wears nearly ended up on the floor."

"And that made you feel good, I suppose."

Lunz laughed and roared and slapped his hand on his thigh. "Oh, Lord, it was a riot! Oh, Lord!"

"So you do have a key to the dorm rooms, then."

"What if I do? There's nothing I want from people here."

"I get it. Just snooping around a little."

"Not for a second. You may not believe it, Schefield, but there is a little larceny in all of us. Yes, in you too! I learned that from Shrink 1 and Shrink 2.

"Damn-well better not go snooping around in my room. Damn-well better not."

"Like I'd want to?"

"Just stay out," I said, targeting a finger on him. I wanted to run him off but hated to do it given the fodder I was getting for my novel. It had a strange way of energizing me enough to scribble a couple more paragraphs.

I took my backpack and set it on my desk. "I'm going to the library to get some studying done. I'm sure as hell not accomplishing much here." I stuffed a book into my pack.

"Library, huh? Yeah, well enjoy it while you can. When we're in charge, out go half the books in that disgusting place. All the crap that's destroying the thinking of people. The books about L, G, B, T, Q…R, S, T, U, V, or whatever. Woke and all that shit. All the books with cockamamie stories about slavery. And, of course, the crap about the Holocaust. All that shit will be out. Great, big, gigantic book burnings just like in Germany in 1933 when they purged the country of all the putrid crap written by Marx and the other degenerate mothers like them."

"From what I can tell, it already started here in the US," I said, sliding another book into my pack.

"Not really. That's just stuff being done out in the burbs where it doesn't amount to a hill of beans. They're just picking the low-hanging fruit. There's a hell of a lot more that'll be done when we get in charge."

I picked up my pack, waved Lunz out the door, and pulled it shut on the way out. Crossing campus, I wondered if I should invite Mona to join me in the library but found my mood much too sour. I did not want to infect her with my attitude.

17

October brought a flash of colors that decorated the campus. The sky was clear, the days shorter. We spent most evenings in Mona's room or in mine tucked under the covers late at night. Our lives were in harmony, more fun than either of us expected. At the end of the quarter our performances in the classroom earned a spot on Dean's list for each of us. But best of all, Krause Lunz seemed to have disappeared.

One evening while lying in bed, Mona ran her finger gently across my forehead and said, "My parents are coming for a visit in a couple of weeks. I'd love it if you could meet them."

"Oh, no," I said. "Is that really a good idea?"

"It's a perfect idea. They already know all about you."

"I don't know…oh, I don't know. I'll be so nervous. I'm not good in those situations. Your parent will wonder why you're dating a jerk like me!"

"No, no, no…they won't. My parents are very sweet people. You'll see. They'll love you. Please…pretty please?"

I sat on the edge of the bed. "What if they hate me?"

Mona took my arm and pulled me toward her and kissed me. "Will that help you decide?"

I climbed back into bed. There were more important things to do now. And anyway, Mona knew quite well I would agree. She had ways to convince me of anything.

We were up in the morning as the call of a rooster came across the quiet slumbering campus from a farm in Huntington Wells. I climbed out of bed, took a shower, and got dressed.

"Off to biology," I said. "No time for coffee, *mon amour*. I'll grab a cup on the way to lecture. Besides, just watching Grayson spin like a gyroscope in front of the room is enough to wake up anyone." I slipped my book into my pack. "Back in an hour or so. You can work here if you want. I won't be long." I raced down the hall and across campus.

It was raining when I emerged from biology. A misty Seattle drizzle settled across campus in pockets of diaphanous fog. I pulled my coat over my head and sped along feeling exalted to be out of class and anxious to return to Mona. I got to my room to find the door open. Mona was gone. Very strange of her to leave and not close the door. I looked around. My writing notebook was on top of my desk. I stared at it. Scrawled across the top in large, jagged letters were the words: HOW COULD YOU DO THIS? YOU ARE A CREEP! A REAL CREEP!

My mind swirled in a blur. I ran down the hall and took the stairs two at a time to the floor below and went to Mona's room and tapped softly on the door but got no reply. I was sure she was inside. Gently pushing the door open, I saw her sitting on the bed, face in her hands.

"Mona, what's going on?" I said gingerly.

She didn't answer. I took two careful steps into the room. "Mona…Mona, what is it?"

She looked up and wiped tears from her cheeks. "I saw what

you did," she said, head in her hands again.

"What I did? What do you mean?"

"I needed a pencil when I was in your room so I opened your desk drawer to get one and there it was, it's about us. About Holly Clarke and Jennifer Rubinstein and me and even Lunz. All of us. You're writing about us. Is that what you've been doing all this time…just getting information to write about? You never said a word. I was so sick when I saw it. You never told me—"

"*That?* Let me explain—"

"There's nothing to explain. I'm sick to my stomach."

"Listen to me for a minute, please."

"I loved you and I thought you loved me. Oh, God, everything has come completely apart." She swept tears from her cheeks. "Oh, God…Oh, God. I'm so sad."

"Please listen. Please."

"There's nothing to hear."

"Please, just try."

She looked at me with the most mournful eyes I had ever seen. All I could do was wait for her to speak. She covered her eyes and said, "It's all over with us, Nick. Oh, I'm mortified. Torn to pieces…"

"Don't say that. That's not true…"

"It is. My life is a mess. I feel like everyone is stalking me. First, I have this…this *creature* who comes into my room and digs through my stuff and leaves disgusting cards about Nazis in my book. And now I have someone who I thought loved me only to find that he's secretly writing stories about me. I just want everyone to leave me alone. Just leave me alone. I want you to go away and never see me again."

"Please, don't say that. Please, Mona, please don't."

"I believed in you. You were the only person I ever truly loved, ever wanted to be with all the time. You made everything in my life good. On those days when I was feeling down, feeling low, wiped out and exhausted, all I had to do was be with you for a minute and everything was better again." She stopped speaking, cleared her eyes, and said, "I thought we were a perfect match, the perfect couple. We were so much alike and so much different. That's why I wanted you to meet my parents. I was so proud of you."

"I would never do anything to hurt you...never. No matter what you think of me now, you are still the most important person in my life," I said. "If you'll just let me explain—"

"Explain what? Explain how you are not like Krause Lunz? Explain that, maybe? Is that what you want to tell me? Well, don't waste your time. You're exactly like him. Go away. Go away and never come back. *Ever.*"

I walked slowly out and returned to my room and fell in my chair. I was tempted to take the tablet with my writing and tear it to shreds, burn it, destroy it. I hated it more than what Krause Lunz had written. I was filled with a sense of dread thinking that I might have lost the one person who meant everything to me. My one true soulmate.

The thought of being a writer now disgusted me. All my fantasies of that were gone. I was tempted to go down to Mona's room to try to convince her that I was not secretly writing about her. To tell her that I would never do that. I wanted to explain that I had not shown what I had written to anyone because it seemed so crude. Barely worth reading. All at once my desire to be a student was swept away.

The night wore on. Darkness filled an empty bitter sky. I sat numbly hoping I would hear Mona tapping on my door and then maybe I could let her know what I was trying to do.

"Oh, God, I really blew it," I uttered. Late at night I curled on the bed and fell into a slow sad sleep.

When I awoke, the sky was dull and gloomy. Misty rain and fog still clung to the campus. I looked at the clock and stumbled out of bed feeling spent and exhausted. So depressed that I was barely able to recall what had happened the night before. It returned to me like a dark and dreadful dream of me standing in Mona's room. The look of despair on her face. Her demand that I never see her again. I could barely bring myself to get out of bed.

I thought about my classes, none of which I had a desire to attend. All I wanted to do was leave Bradford and never come back. Never to sit in class, to study, to learn. Worst of all, I had Psychology later in the day, the only class I shared with Mona. I trembled just thinking of it. Maybe she would be there. Maybe she will have recovered from her anger. Or maybe she will ignore me as if I were no different from the dozens of others in the class. Treat me like I was invisible. Come in, take notes, leave.

Time crept by. I struggled through the morning. Made a cup of coffee but drank almost none of it. Sat at my desk and tried to work but couldn't. Skipped lunch. At three-thirty, I tucked my psychology text into my pack and made a fretful walk out the door to my four o'clock class. *What if she's there?* I thought, crossing campus in a daze. *What if she's there and ignores me? Hates me? I'll be devastated.* I walked into the classroom and sat at the desk I always occupied for the lecture. Mona was not in the room. Would she come in and sit next to me as she always had done? I twiddled my pencil. Dropped it on the floor. Picked it up.

Twiddled again. Students filtered in. Barely two minutes before class began, Mona came in and took a seat on the far side of the room, never looking at me. I didn't remember a word of the lecture. Not even sure I took notes. When the class was over I stumbled across campus and returned to my room and sat in a stupor for hours. Minutes ticked endlessly.

A week went by. I barely remembered any of it. Day after day, Mona avoided me. Day after day, it became clear that our brief enchanting relationship was falling into the past. My usually good appetite dwindled to nothing. Finally, one evening I managed to go to the cafeteria. The choices were once again familiar, all the standard offerings I normally found enjoyable. I went through the line, selected an entree, and took a seat at a table alone and lonely. I hadn't noticed at first but glancing across the room my eyes fell on a table where Mona sat with a male student. My heart came to a stop. What a grim omen! I toyed with my food. She had not seen me. She seemed happy, laughing in a way I had seen her do a million times when she was with me. I swept moisture from the edge of my eye. Was she happy? Happy the way I remembered? I had no way of knowing. She always spread joy to everyone she was with. I could not bear to be there any longer. Having lost my appetite, I got up and quietly left.

In my room, I took a sheet of paper from my desk. I would tell Mona how I felt. Would tell her I had no intention of hurting her and that I hoped she would forgive me. My eyes blurred as I wrote. Three times I stopped, walked to the window, and viewed the age-old buildings of Bradford to regain my composure. When I finished writing, I read what I had written and folded it and slipped it into an envelope. My pulse throbbed in my neck as I walked down the hall.

Mona's door was closed. I hoped she would be alone when she found the note. I wedged it into the crack of the door and went back to my room and dropped into my chair, exhausted. At eight thirty by the clock on the wall, I closed my eyes and fell into a numb half-sleep.

Two hours later, a tap came on the door. I knew immediately it was Mona. Nervous and jittery, I leapt to my feet and opened the door, Mona stood in the hall with the most remorseful look. "Can I…" she whispered.

"Yes, yes," I said. I had no idea what she wanted. More excoriation, or maybe forgiveness? It almost did not matter; I was happy just seeing her, if only briefly.

She stood for a moment saying nothing then sat on the bed. "I read your letter," she said, resting her hands on her lap.

"Can I sit down?" I asked.

She said, "Maybe I…"

Afraid she might stop talking and walk out, I said, "You see, I truly was not trying to write secretly about you. I don't know how else to say it. What happened was—" I stopped for a second and caught my breath. "When I came to Bradford I thought I would take up a major that I could use to get a job as a diplomat someday." I told her about my father's ambassador friend and how much he liked his job and how it seemed like a good profession. "But the more I thought about it, the less exciting it sounded. I've always had an interest in writing. So…I guess I wildly believed I would become a writer."

Mona looked at me and chuckled softly.

"And that's when I started to…I had this fantasy that I would be a writer…a great writer of fiction." I laughed. "Of course, I'm quite sure that will never happen. But anyway, I decided to try writing a novel. And so, I don't know what more I can say. I haven't gotten very far along and what I've written so far sucks. I was too embarrassed to let anyone read it. When it comes to writing, they say you should write about what you know. That's what they say. So that's what I did. They never said if you do that a whole lot of people are going to be mad as hell."

Mona smiled. She leaned over and kissed me gently. "Oh, I missed you," she said. "And, no, I don't hate you."

"Mona, Mona, Mona, I missed you so much. I felt as though my life had come apart…completely apart. Torn to shreds."

"I thought about you all the time," Mona said. "I felt so alone. This evening a guy I know asked if I wanted to get something to eat at the cafeteria. Oh, he's a nice guy and all, but the whole time, all I could do was think of you. All I wanted to do was be with you. I wanted to be there sitting with you."

She kissed me again.

We rolled in bed for hours and then late at night fell into a soft and peaceful sleep until the first light of dawn. Later, we went to the Union for coffee and headed to class and agreed to meet in my room.

As I unloaded books from my pack in the afternoon, Mona said, "I want to tell you that I hope you don't stop writing your book. I want you to keep going. And in all honesty, I liked what you wrote…from what I read, at least." She scrunched her nose and said, "I think you really nailed Lunz."

I put my arms around her waist. "Oh, Lord, I was so disgusted. I almost tore it to pieces. It might have been a good thing if I had. All I can tell you is that every time I go back and read it, I realize how much I need to learn. At least if I tore it to shreds, I could start over with something else and this time leave all of us out."

"I think you should continue with it. Maybe you found out what you really want to do in life. Maybe you *will* be a great writer of fiction. I hope so. Me? I don't know, I'm still struggling to figure out what I want to do. Today, one thing. Tomorrow, something else."

18

The week was long and arduous. I bombed on the biology test, coming away with a low C due to endless days fraught with the emotional turbulence when Mona left. It pulled all the wind from my sails. And though that was now over, I had to plug through an all-night cram for Grayson's test. A class in which information gushed out of the mighty Grayson like a category five hurricane tearing across a coastal beach. I was convinced this would be my last biology class at Bradford, that a career in medicine was not my calling—a page in my life that I was happy to flip. Mona, as usual, buzzed through her classes, acing two tests and getting a rave evaluation on a presentation in anthropology.

We went to the Union Saturday evening. A band was playing. The lights were dimmed. The room was gregarious and lively. It felt great to be there with Mona. An eclectic repertoire of music filled the air. SKA, hip-hop, rifts of twelve-bar blues sent legions of students out to dance. People came from all parts of campus. We gathered with a group of friends: Holly Clarke and Jennifer Rubinstein and an ever-growing constellation of students who collected around Mona, the natural-born extrovert. The Union sold beer to those of age. One-third of the crowd was sober, one-third was tipsy, one-third wobbled and teetered.

Mona grabbed my hand and drew me to the dance floor. People rocked and gyrated and bobbed and jammed tightly in all forms of human motion. The room exploded with sound. Half an hour went by. We walked to the edge of the room hot and happy. I wiped perspiration from my forehead. The long week was behind us. How glad I was.

"God, I'm horny. You drive me nuts," I said to Mona as we stood by the wall. Mona laughed. She kissed me and gave a look that said fun was in store.

More people packed into the Union. The band was getting ready to break. I glanced around the room. Lots of people I knew plus one I hoped not to see. Standing by the door was Krause Lunz.

"Don't look now. Guess who's here?" I warned.

Mona looked instinctively over. "Pretend he's not here. He'll probably leave us alone," she said, as if an angry wasp was buzzing our heads.

"He's got a couple of his buddies with him. NPP creeps, I'm sure."

Lunz shambled his way across the floor to where Holly Clarke and Jennifer Rubinstein were. He grabbed Holly by the arm and yanked her toward him and slushed a kiss on her. She threw him back, looking as though she was about to plug him with all she had.

"Maybe he'll just wander around and leave," Mona said. "I doubt that this is his idea of a good time. Too much fun for a lowlife like Lunz." We turned a shoulder to him hoping to escape his sight. Seeing us, he jammed himself intrusively across the room, a coterie of four close behind. "Well, well, well…and guess who I have found?" he lipped.

I looked at Lunz and glanced quickly at the others with him. There on the arm of each was a tattoo just like Lunz had shown me in my room. One of his henchmen had his hair combed across his forehead in a distinctly Hitleresque way. It was clear they were all juiced.

"Yes, look who I have come across. It's my friend Nickie and his dear little sweetheart Monickie." He let out a grotesque laugh. "My two dorm compadres…Nickie and Monickie." The contingent with Lunz laughed in little less than a controlled shriek, causing students around us to turn and stare.

"How about you just leave us alone," I demanded, shooing him off with my hand while trying to control the anger that welled in me. "We didn't come here to be pestered by the likes of you, Lunz! Find someone else to irritate." I shooed him again.

Lunz puffed his chest and started to speak but lost his balance and tipped awkwardly back. He was caught by one of his foot soldiers who stood him up like a plastic toy. "The likes of you…how cute," he bellowed on wobbly feet. He looked around the room. "My, what a jamboree we have here. The Brad really knows how to treat the kiddies, doesn't it? A band and even some brew. Are we having fun yet? We didn't come here for that stuff, of course," he said, waving his arms spastically and pantomiming like he was dancing. "We came to knock down some brewskies. The price is right, hey why not?" He dumped what was left in his cup on the floor and kicked the cup away and laughed and turned to Mona. His eyes rolled up and down and across her, head to foot, top to bottom. "*Wow-wee! Whoa doggie!* I *love* those skin-tight jeans of yours. Oh…my…God! They fit you snug as hell. I can't stand it! I bet it took forever to squeeze into them. I bet it's going to take even longer to squeeze out of them," he said, in a voice rocked with vulgarity. "What do you think, Nickie—old buddy? Hot stuff, huh? *Wow!*"

I had enough. With a full four inches in height on Lunz, I grabbed him by his shirt and shoved him away. He slid onto the floor and clumsily tried to climb to his feet. Students watched. He tried to right himself but slipped onto his side again. A member of his group grabbed him by his arm and propped him up precariously. The shock of what happened seemed to have settled into Lunz's sozzled cortex. Standing on shaky legs, swaying back and forth, he attempted to lunge at me. With little effort, I deflected the attack. One of his goons grabbed him. "Out, *Mein Herr*, let's go, let's go," he said, snatching Lunz by his belt and yanking him away. Vainly refusing to quit, Lunz leaned forward and dove at me. I caught him on the jaw with a sharp right cross, knocking him into the arms of his pack. I shook my fist in pain. Blood drizzled from Lunz's nose. *"Mein Herr, Mein Herr! Out, out!"* To no avail, Lunz again tried to dive at me but was pulled away. They plowed through the crowd knocking people aside like empty milk bottles and left the Union.

I rubbed my knuckles. I might have broken Lunz's face but my knuckles seemed to be in equally bad shape. Disgusted by the whole affair, I said, "See, that bastard Lunz did it again. He ruined the whole night."

"No, no. No matter what Lunz does, we will be fine, *l'amoureux*. He will *never* ruin our time together. Never! We can't let him," Mona said, leading me out to dance.

19

Days passed. I had not heard a peep from Krause Lunz despite having passed his room many times on my way in and out of the dorm. Perhaps he had indeed checked out. He never went to class, so he claimed. He had finished writing his grandiose political rhapsody. And by his own admission he had more important work to do with the NPP than to waste his time putzing around Bradford.

This bounty of goodwill prompted me to leave my door open. I was mostly content with my progress in school, though each day biology had become more grueling and less appealing. I vowed never again to get caught in a course laden with equations, formulas, and cell cycles. The thrill of learning about the ecclesiastical designs of nature no longer interested me, Grayson's mesmerizing lectures notwithstanding. Even the struggle to get a few worthy paragraphs onto a page of my fledgling novel gave me more pleasure. I was now convinced that this was where my future lay.

But, of course, nothing in life goes quite as smoothly as we hoped and, sure enough, a beautiful and sophisticated morning was soon shattered by the presence of Krause Lunz at my door.

He entered with the swagger of a cat that has taken over the house as he strode pompously across the room to the window. I was shocked that he would ever again make a showing after our encounter in the Union.

"Just who I want to see," I said. "I've got a bone to pick with you."

"Pick away," Lunz calmly replied, glancing inertly across the campus as if nothing had happened between us.

"I didn't appreciate one damn bit what you said to Mona in the Union."

Lunz shrugged. "Had a bit too much grog, I suppose. Nothing more than that. Thought it was a pretty good compliment, if you need to know."

"Keep your compliments to yourself."

Lunz turned and gave a foolish salute off the top of his brow and returned to Bradford. "Probably thought I was gone, didn't you? That's the scuttle around campus, or so I hear. So says Berman. The guy is a walking bucket of rumors. There's not a spoken word here in the hallowed halls of Bradford that escapes him. It's a legacy of their time in Germany. They store everything up as ammo in case they need to accuse someone of mistreating them is what I'm saying. It goes back to their days in Krautland."

"First of all, that's a goddamn disgusting thing to say, Lunz. Second of all, I thought you don't believe what happened back then…the Holocaust I mean."

"I don't. Just saying. Ah…fuggit—"

My calculation was that the less I said the sooner Lunz would find his way to the door. Yet I knew that the more I wanted him out, the longer he would stay. Another game of wits on his part.

"Up to my ears in NPP work. I'm actually starting to like this politics garbage. Everything is rolling along perfectly. Better than perfect, in fact. Horace Crockett—the election is in the bag. Let's see." He checked the date on his watch. "Two weeks almost to the day now and the roly-poly hick down there in Bama becomes the first ever NPP in Congress. The first fascist. This is how the movement gets moving." He looked at me and said, "See, it's like a wave. Almost nothing at first, and then bigger and bigger. That's how movements like this, like the NPP, how they get their start."

"And most likely the last out of the gate for your NPP party," I said. "No one's going to buy the crap you guys are peddling."

"Just one of many more candidates to come. You'll see. It'll be splashed all over the pages of the *Times*. Huge articles about it. Just wait."

"Too busy to follow."

"Doesn't matter. It'll hit the news like ten points on the Richter come the fifth of November. I guarantee! And like I said, all the grumpy bitches on the left-wing cable stations are going to wet their big baggy knickers right there live and in person before the camera."

"Don't watch the news…do you see a TV in here?"

"Tangsley will probably freak, too. Dumb as he is, he's got enough gray matter to know it's a premonition of big changes to come."

"Oh really. And then what?"

"And then this *grand*…this *grand* country of yours will finally end up where it was destined to be from the moment of its birth. In a great big dumpster, hopelessly trashed forever and ready for a bright new beginning."

"You've got a helluva long way to go before that happens."

"Bet you don't even know how many people there are in the House of Representatives, do you?"

"The House of Representatives? Let me see. Let me take a wild stab at it," I said, pretending to be flummoxed by Lunz's query. "Hmm…hmm, could it be that there are four hundred and thirty-five?"

"Nice guess. Nice damn guess," Lunz said. "We've done the math, yep. The NPP is not a bunch of idiots and morons like you seem to think. We've got it all calculated down to the very last person. We know exactly which House seats we can flip. A bunch of redneck ones down below the Mason-Dixon. We'll grab those real fast one after another. Tick, tick, tick. And the Congressional rat holes up in no man's land. You know, joints like the Dakotas, Wyoming, Montana, Idaho. We'll pick off quite a few slots in those places next time around. It's going to be a cake walk once we get rolling."

"One or two people in Congress. You think that's going to make a difference?"

"Time to educate Schefield. All it takes is one or two in the House or the Senate. Know why? Because they'll be right smack between the Democrat and Republican mullet heads. That's why. They'll kiss our ass because they know they need our votes. And when we want something from them, they'll leap to it. One hand washes the other…been like that from time immemorial."

When he saw I was about ready to escort him to the door, he glanced conspicuously at his watch and bungled his way down the hall.

After Lunz left I went to the window and looked at the pale blue sky. The low morning fog had vanished. The buildings appeared like megaliths put down by some ancient giant who roamed the earth eons ago. I opened the window an inch. A whimpering breeze coursed into the room. I had no classes for hours. I would go for a long run in the hopes of breaking my thoughts free from Lunz's words that seemed to hang in my room like a bitter foul odor that permeated everything. I put on a t-shirt, shorts, and running shoes, went outside, stretched, did a few push-ups and sit-ups. I knew Mona was in class and would not be out for hours. Leaning forward, I took to a path that led to the edge of campus and started down the sleepy streets of Huntington Wells until I arrived at a simple country road devoid of people and traffic. The cathedral of trees bragged of October joy. One last and grand adventure on their part before ending the year in quiet hebetude not to be awakened again for months to come.

I ran perhaps five miles and stopped at a small stream that followed the road. Likely the same water that flowed through Samuels' Park where Mona and I had picnicked. Schools of small fish again gathered and darted haphazardly through the crystal water near the bank. I watched and wondered why it was that they had been granted such simple pleasure in their brief stay on the planet. I wiped sweat from my brow and across the back of my neck as I sat on a rock under a vast and consumptive sky. My thoughts took me to Mona. Being in love with her was pure ecstasy. "Ah, *mon chéri*," I said to the fickle wind that rustled the painted leaves and to a lone mockingbird that warbled in the tree above me. Who besides myself was listening to its enchanting song, I wondered.

An autumn bloom spread forth around me. Purple anise hyssop, orange day lilies, red and yellow helenium, white garden phlox. I stretched out on the soft grass. High above a pair of eagles soared and turned and dipped, watching for the telltale movement of life far below. A reckless squirrel or hare, fish in the nearby river perhaps.

I thought about my novel, if one could call it that. Indeed, it was becoming a struggle. Each word had to be pried one by one from the clutch of the muse—and a stingy muse it was. Days came when I almost fell back to my plans of a career in government. How bad could it be? Predictable, if nothing else. The thought of writing swell novels on some perfect island in the Caribbean drinking rum and fishing from a long wooden cabin cruiser seemed more and more like a grandiose dream. What a rollercoaster my brief time at Bradford had been. Classes were a challenge and despite what Lunz said, Tangsley was a brilliant and gifted teacher who delivered information eloquently and with grace in full round sentences. As did Grayson in Biology, if perhaps with long non-stop explosions of information and boundless detail. The lectures in all my classes—Psychology, English Literature—were likewise delivered with great elan. I pushed hard to do well in every course. In that way, I was my father's son.

I watched the clouds form and shape and spread and evaporate. Artwork in the sky. Next Monday would bring the semester break. If Lunz's predictions came true he would be heading out to help Horace Crockett in his last-minute push to get elected. Perhaps I would get a brief reprieve from his endless tirades. I thought about Lunz's prognostication of Crockett's success at the polls and realized it was now certain to happen. Already, op-eds were surfacing in the *Times* and *The Washington Post* trying to dissect how the country's first neo-Nazi, the first proud white nationalist, would earn a seat in Congress. That it would happen was no longer a hypothetical proposition, a wild possibility. Horace Crockett, this man who for months had become an apostle of hatred, would soon be emplaced in America's most hallowed of all buildings merely because of the right of every American to cast a ballot for candidates of their choice no matter how reprehensible they might be.

Did I remember Lunz mentioning that Crockett had offered him a position as a senior congressional staffer in his office? Chief of Staff, possibly? Good…go and stalk the halls of the Capitol and pour forth the sludge of your troubled mind to the media—a media that would tag along behind Crockett as they did with the other malignant members of Congress who fed their egos on the endless attention they were getting. A media that followed them like doting mothers behind whiny two-year-olds trying to keep them from yanking the curtains off the windows. How they loved it, these newly minted politicians. How important it made them feel. *Strange it is*, I thought, *that a person can go from being a wretch of no consequence to a rarified member of Congress—whether good or bad, benevolent or inherently evil—merely by the cast of a few votes.*

An hour passed. I picked myself up and jogged back to the dorm with even less enthusiasm than when I left.

The following week brought fall semester break. It was good to be out of the classroom. The campus was almost empty. Students had left. Skiing in Vermont. To the beaches in Florida and the Gulf Coast. Home to visit families. I was stuck on campus, you might say. I had little desire to spend a week at home.

Mona's parents arrived for a two-day visit. She insisted that I meet them and, as nervous as I was, I found them to be exactly like Mona—kind and gentle and pleasant. A pleasure to be with. It was evident whence Mona had acquired her many good qualities.

We went one afternoon to Ponzo's Pizzeria in Huntington Wells, the place that Mona and I discovered the night we saw *Fat Ham*. We liked their version of pizza and had made many visits to it since. Sitting in the small restaurant—six tables covered with red-checked tablecloths, a bar with barely five stools, a wide-screen TV on the wall for baseball and hockey—Mona's father said, "Vell, Nick, I understand zat you want to work in za government. Let me tell you, zat eez a good sing to do. And Mona said you might try to go into zee diplomatic corps. Eez zat right? Vell, eet eez good if you do. I know many people who work in the State Department and zey all like what zey do." He went on to describe his work. It sounded almost enticing despite my inherent dislike of the legal profession.

I said, "Well, my interests may have changed a bit."

"Oooh?"

"Yes, Nick wants to be a writer. He's going to be great writer of fiction," Mona boasted.

I burst into laughter. "Well, I don't know how *great* I'll be."

"And this is an excellent choice, too," Mona's mother said. "Being a writer is a very good profession. I'm glad you want to go into the arts. Mona probably told you I work at The National Gallery."

"She's one of the art curators there," Mona added proudly.

"When I was in graduate school studying art history, I spent some time at the Art Institute of Chicago. It is a wonderful place. But I was there in the middle of winter. I think the temperature was below zero every day. At least that's what my bones believed.

It was so *cold*. While I was at the Institute, I studied all forms of art from the Masters to the Impressionists to American Folk Art. That's where I got hooked on folk art. It's actually a very elaborate style, a lot more complicated than people think. Sometimes a canvas can have dozens of scenes with all kinds of activities happening with all kinds of people. And so, when Mona's father and I moved to DC, a position came up as curator of the Folk Art section. I applied and got the job."

"And even though I know almost nothing about art, I love to hear about it," Mona's father said.

Later in the day, we climbed into the car Mona's parents rented and went for a trip through the countryside under a canopy of trees in radiant autumn display. The next evening, they insisted I join them for dinner at an elegant French restaurant in the heart of Huntington Wells.

20

The one-week break from schoolwork was good but it did not seem to be nearly enough. Before I knew it I was again submerged in assignments. I had made little progress on my novel despite plans to grind out as much as possible during the time away from class. No such luck.

I had three tests within the span of a week. A trick, it seemed, invented by some cantankerous administrator. Give them a couple of days off and then come at them with both barrels loaded. *Cest la vie*, as Mona liked to say.

A week went by, then another. I heard not hide-nor-hair from Krause Lunz. October flipped to November. The 5th of the month arrived. With little success, I tried not to think about it even to the point of refusing to make my customary stop at the library for a quick read of the *Times* on the way back from class. But of course, I knew that no matter what, when the day arrived it would hold as much darkness for America as when the stock market tumbled in 1929.

As usual, I passed Lunz's room several times while heading through the dorm. His door was shut—not a sound from the raucous Nazi. Neither Holly Clarke nor Jennifer Rubinstein nor

Mona had heard a peep from him. Could it be that he was finally gone? Off to spread his torrent of evil tidings around Washington?

But luck I did not have. I was moving quickly through the pages of Tangsley's history book when I heard a rap on the door. The rap of Kraus Wilhelm Lunz, to be sure. There he stood flush with exhilaration. Every millimeter of his face and neck radiated a pink glow.

"What do you think of *that*, Schefield, old boy? *We goddamn did it!*" he wailed. "Did what every fuck head said was impossible. Killed the opposition, buried them. It was total devastation for the dork the Democrats put up. Even worse for the jackass the Republicans put up. What a damn blowout." Lunz said from deep in his chest. "Mind if I come in?"

"I think you already did."

He laughed. "Yes, seems so." He swept hair from his eyes. "*Did you read about it? Did you?*"

I shook my head. I had not. I didn't need to. No point in it.

"The media is freaked. Not all of them, of course. Just the left-wing doofuses on MSNBC and CNN, those places. They may all be a bunch of twisted lefties but a couple of them are cuties. You know the ones I mean." He rattled off a name. "Well, everyone on cable is going flat out nuts at the Crockett victory. Talking about it like it's the nineteen thirties when Hitler snatched the reins from the hands of the worn-out Weimar Republic. It's been a big freakout by all the liberal pinheads. I told you this was going to happen. Told you so. You didn't believe me." Lunz said, barely able to catch his breath.

"I think you're way overplaying it," I said.

"Oh, there are a few crackerjacks spouting out sensible stuff.

Praising the success of what happened. The Fox News crowd, for example. They've all been drooling nonstop like Pavlov's dogs since Crockett got elected."

"Like I said, I haven't been following it. I've got a million and one things to do yet this semester and—"

"Crockett offered me a job as part of his Congressional staff," Lunz reminded me, dissing my comment.

"Take it."

"You wouldn't be trying to get rid of me, would you?" He gurgled a long laugh. "It's a thought but I haven't decided yet. Working for Crockett, I mean. Might consider it if I can be the big cheese. You know, chief cook and bottle washer, that sort of thing. I'd give the say-so about who gets to talk to Crockett. Plan his daily schedule. Get him up to speed for whatever committees he's on. He's hoping for the House Judiciary Committee. That would be tits, for sure. It's a long shot but possible. You might not know it but he's a lawyer. Country lawyer, true, but lawyer just the same. The kind who knows a lot of shit about nothing but a lot of shit about the important stuff. The kind of lawyer who's got the judge in his back pocket. Someone who can get nine or ten in the slammer for a crappy little misdemeanor depending upon what shade you happen to be...if you get my drift. Crockett would be a terror on the Judiciary Committee. You can tell that just from talking to him. Ah, so what! All that matters is that we got our guy in the big house. Got him a room in the holy Capitol building with all the other sanctimonious slobs who think they know how to run this country. A country that's totally fubar. Totally!"

"You have a stellar opinion of this Crocket guy."

Lunz's head bobbled with laughter. "Truth is, I doubt that

I'll take the job. I prefer working on NPP campaigns, especially now that we cracked the nut on the whole political process. I'm pretty damn good at it, this campaign stuff. It takes a certain type of person. You need to know which way the political winds are blowing. We've got a special election coming up soon to fill a vacant Congressional slot in Wyoming. Dude fell off his horse onto his goddamn head, broke his neck and died. Stupid asshole! They'll be holding an election for the seat soon. Fuggit, if nothing else, I'll probably like Wyoming a whole lot better than Bama. Or going to Washington to work for a yokel like Crockett. Doesn't sound all that exciting, does it? Working for some redneck even if he did manage to get his chubby fanny sent to Congress."

"Why do I get the feeling there are lots of people who would support the NPP in Wyoming?"

"It has its share of white nationalists…be sure of that. They're a bunch of real independent jocks up there…hate the government with a passion. Just the kind of joint where we can *rope* another NPP dude into Congress. No pun intended."

I was getting ready to push Lunz out the door when he said, "I've got something to show you. Brought back a little memento, a souvenir from Bama." He waved for me to follow him to his room.

"Lunz, for Christ's sake, I'm busy."

Lunz snickered.

"This better be good."

When we got to his room he went to his desk and opened the drawer and pulled out what appeared to be a bumper sticker and handed it to me.

"Get a load of this. Going to slap this baby on the wall right there next to my cherished Iron Cross."

I stared at what he had handed me. Joke or serious, I was disgusted.

IF I HAD KNOWN THIS WAS GONNA HAPPEN I'D HAVE PICKED MY OWN DAMN COTTON!

I threw it back at Lunz. It sailed toward him and landed on the floor. "You think that's funny, do you? Is that what you think? You've got a real sick sense of humor, Lunz, you know that? A real sick sense of humor. That thing is revolting."

"Got it in rural Bama at an old gas station-cigar store. If nothing else those rubes know how to do it right."

"Well, then maybe that's where you should be, down in Alabama," I said, starting for the door. "If I ever see that piece of shit on the wall in here, I'll tear it to shreds!" As I was leaving, I turned and said, "And don't you dare let Monique see that!"

Lunz glared at me in silence. Something told me he might do exactly that now that he saw how it angered me.

I returned to my room. Once again, Lunz had managed to invade the solitude of my mind. I hoped Mona would stop by. Her presence was like a balm that soothed my nerves. My biggest worry, of course, was that Lunz would flaunt his latest acquisition and flash it around to whomever came by, pretending it was a joke while he gloried in every second of it. I knew sooner or later Holly Clarke would probably see it. Not that she would be in his room for a connubial visit. From what I could tell, those days were over despite the fiction Lunz tried to spread about him and Holly. Even so, he had ways of snaring people with his crays. But my worst fear was that Mona would see it. I knew that she already had her share of painful experiences of that kind. One more she did not need. Were Lunz to pin the sticker to the wall as he claimed he would, should I rip it off and destroy it as I threatened? I slumped in my soft chair and closed my eyes. When would this end? Some people are inherently evil, most are generally good, but none are both. After endless hours in the presence of Lunz I began to wonder what formed the underpinnings of his deep-seated animosities, his hatred for people who from what I could tell had never done anything to drive his prejudices. I stared out the window where a steel-gray sky bunkered a chilling premonition of winter.

Late in the evening I got a call from my father's housekeeper with bad news. She told me my father had passed away. It happened just after dinner. He was not feeling well. He went into the living room and after he sat down he began having chest pains. An ambulance came out and brought him to the hospital but by the time they got there his heart had stopped. They were unable to resuscitate him. I told her I was grateful for getting in touch with me and said I would be on the first flight home in the morning.

Memories of my father filled my thoughts. He was a kind man. Everything he did, he did with good intentions. I wondered if he had been a happy man. Peculiar that I considered that about someone I had been around my whole life. Quiet and reserved, it was difficult to know what emotions trickled through him. So, I concluded he was happy in his own way, and in the long run that was all that mattered.

I suppose it might be said that I was now without parents. Too old to be an orphan but alone just the same. Alone with no siblings and no close relatives. I did not feel sad about that. It's hard to miss what you never had.

In an hour's time, I walked down to Mona's room and gave a soft tap on her door. I told her about the news from home. She hugged me with a sense of bereavement as deep as mine as she held me close in her arms.

"I'll be back in a few days," I said. "I suspect I'll need to make some arrangements for...for whatever needs to be done. I will get in touch with my father's lawyer. I assume he will be able to handle most of the details." I gave Mona a kiss and said, "I'll let you know how things are going." I started for the door then turned and said, "I love you."

"And you, *ma très chère*."

21

Sitting by the window of the plane, my thoughts were filled with every memory of my youth. Days of living in a comfortable suburb on the outskirts of Chicago. My father, the depth of his blue eyes, the smile he rarely wore. Will I ever live in Chicago again? Would I want to live in Chicago again? I watched the green-brown squares and rectangles of farmland below that took on the appearance of a luxurious quilt spread across the land. It had once been good to me but now I felt that I had only been a sojourner through the great stretch of concrete that is America's second city. It seemed foreign and unusual now. As mysterious to me as it is to those who stand along Michigan Avenue like small insects staring up at the towering steel and mortar headstones of man's creativity as they reach for the sky. Would there be a day when after mankind has sucked the last breath of soluble oxygen off the planet, when we have finally done that, leading to our own extinction, would nothing be left behind but those gargantuan structures as mute as the faces on Easter Island? If that were to happen would others a million years from now, two million years, curiously question why such relics had been deposited along the edge of the great blue waters of Lake

Michigan? This, I considered as the farms and countryside of America slipped below me.

The plane swung over Lake Michigan as we descended through dense gray clouds that hovered above Chicago. I looked at the precise layout of the city cut into squares like its famous pizza. Streets divided into a perfect design: north by south, east by west. The tires of the plane screeched on the tarmac at O'Hare. I grabbed my duffel and left the concourse. The air outside was cold. Unlike the weather in Huntington Wells, it had a sharp snap of winter in its teeth. Moist dank air from the lake. I got a cab for Hinsdale.

Elvira met me at the door when I got to the house. She told me she was sorry about my father and asked if there was anything she could get me. I thanked her. I set my bag down, not knowing where to go, what to do. I felt like a stranger in a place I had occupied most of my life. I had an instinct to sit in the living room and listen to the stillness I had once known all too well. But rather, I started through the house room by room knowing it would be my last visit to it.

"I have been in touch with Ben," Elvira said. "He pulled your father's will and is going to look it over. He said he will take care of the whole matter and will put the house up for sale. I assumed that's what you wanted."

"Yes…thank you. What about you, Elvie? Will you be able to get by now?"

"Oh, yes. I'll be fine. Your father was a good man to work for. I'll probably go and live with my sister in Minnesota for a while."

Standing in the kitchen my eyes immediately landed on the martini shaker my father used every night—sterling and engraved with his initials. I never knew if it was a gift, or if someone had it engraved for him. It brought a smile to me.

Each room was filled with memories that seemed to be embedded into the walls and the oak and teak woodwork of the elegant house like the telltale vapors of holy incense that decorate the pietistic chambers of Catholic churches. I went to my bedroom, looked around for a minute, then lay on the bed for quite a while. A page of my life had now turned. Though I was sorry that my father had moved on—as it were—I was nonetheless content to be adjoining the next phase of what life held for me. I thought about this. In a crazy concocted way I realized that, like the novel I was struggling to write, life comes with chapters and episodes and scenes, some easily offered, some with inherent challenges.

I must have been deep in thought longer than I realized. Elvira stuck her head in the door. "Everything okay, Nick?"

"Yeah, it's fine, Elvie," I said.

"Anything I can get you?"

"No, I'm fine. Thanks."

When I came downstairs, Elvira had placed a book of photographs and snapshots on the dining room table.

"Your father kept this in his closet. I suppose you will want it," she said.

I opened the book and paged through it. Some of the pictures I had seen before. Many were new to me. Each one stored neatly in perfect chronological order beginning with snapshots of my father and my mother on their wedding day. These, more than any of the rest, stole my attention. I had never seen such a happy look on my father's face. It glowed. I now knew better than ever why his days with my mother were likely the best of his life. My mother's face flashed a radiant smile—one that I barely remembered. Perhaps most of my memories of her came from a time when she was already ill.

The remaining days were filled with the dreary necessities of closing the final stage of my father's life. I had an urge to go into the Loop and spend time at places I was once familiar with. I'm not sure why. Possibly because I knew it would be the last time I would do so for a long while.

I had coffee at a café on Hinsdale Avenue across from the Burlington station and sat for a while watching the trains as they whistled back and forth between Chicago and Aurora. A deluge of memories flooded my thoughts. Even though it had been only a few months since I left Chicago, it seemed longer. No doubt, the passing of my father and the separation of the last tangible connection to those days added to that feeling. From the table by the window in the café, I could see the sky—tarnished blue and pewter gray. A more typical winter Chicago sky there was not. The lines of the famous poem by Carl Sandburg about the city came to mind. Words that were as true today as when he wrote them more than a century ago.

"*...stormy, husky, brawling. City of the Big Shoulders...*"

I sent Mona a text and a selfie. She immediately sent a text back asking how everything was going. I told her I had spoken briefly with my father's lawyer and that everything was moving along. My father, being the precise and diligent person he was, made for easy closure to his estate. I told her I loved her and missed her and couldn't wait to be with her at Bradford again.

The morning trains to the city run promptly one after another. On any other day, I would have avoided the milk trains, the ones that stopped at every station along the way. But on that morning it did not matter to me. A part of me wanted to see as much of the old city as possible on my way to the Loop. A city I once knew like I knew my name.

I bought a ticket and climbed on the train and took a seat on the top deck. The conductor came through the car. "Tickets." He reached up, punched my ticket, and stuck it on the clip by my seat. A routine that had been done on the commuter trains since the days of steam locomotives. I thought about my father, how he rode the train at the same time to and from work each day reading the newspaper as the train swayed on the rails like a small craft at sea.

The suburbs flickered past the window one after another: Western Springs, La Grange, Brookfield, Riverside, Berwyn, Cicero. Ethnic churches with pinpoint steeples. Catholic, Orthodox, Protestant. Old streets where shops and bakeries and delis sold dark ryes and Russian black breads and kolaches and pierogies and other tantalizing delights. The neighborhood ball fields of summer little leagues. The two-flats and the four-flats of the immigrants from dozens of Eastern European countries. The Italians and Irish. The amalgam of groups that formed the core of Sandburg's poem. The factories and stockyards and meat-packing companies that employed them.

The train crawled into Union Station and rolled to a stop. I walked east on Jackson Boulevard into the Loop, crossed the Chicago River, turned south for a block onto Van Buren Street and passed the Chicago Board of Trade. I could sense my father's lost presence inside. I stopped for a while, barely more than a minute, then moved on, arriving at my destination exactly at noon and entered the elegant Russian Tea Time Restaurant at 77 Adams Street. Hands down, my father's favorite place to dine in all Chicago.

The hostess led me to a table near the wall in a room as perfectly decorated with posh red curtains and gilded chandeliers as if expecting the Czar and his court to enter at any moment. I looked the menu over but knew I would have what had been my father's favorite meal, which like most things in his life was never modified. Siberian Baerii sturgeon caviar served with blintzes, chopped onion, egg salad, sour cream and drawn butter, for openers. A cup of Ukrainian borscht as a second. An entrée of beef stroganoff. I took the meal leisurely as my father always had done. And, of course, tea at the end.

After a long slow meal I paid the bill, which normally would have made me cringe just to look at it. But on that day of remembrance the cost made no difference whatsoever. Content, I left and began out into the Loop again. *Where to now*, I thought. Barely a block away was the Chicago Art Institute directly across Michigan Avenue. The air coming down the avenue had a mood of an impending snowfall that might explode onto the city at any moment. I walked up the steps that were defended by a pair of large stone lions.

There was no doubt where I would go, what I would visit— the requisite stops I always made during my visits to the museum. The Impressionist gallery, Monet's seminal collection of *Stacks of Wheat*, the earthy image of *The Arrival of the Normandy Train, Gare Saint-Lazare*. Everything by Sisley, Pissarro, Morisot, Degas, Manet, and the others. Van Gogh's empty, lonely, subdued *Bedroom at Arles*. I could devote an afternoon to any or all of those. And then the American classics: *Nighthawks* by Edward Hopper. *American Gothic* by Grant Wood painted in 1930 in Eldon, Iowa, the heartland of America. On and on.

Before I knew it, almost three hours had passed and I had yet to make it to my planned kismet—the Folk Art exhibit. Entering the exhibit, the room came alive as if all the images in all the paintings were suddenly animated, marching across canvases like creatures in Walt Disney's *Fantasia*. I realized why Mona's mother had found the art so invigorating. Each canvas told a story in the most vivid way. Every painting breathed. The snow was cold. The heat coming down from the summer sun was warm. Streams bubbled and gurgled. Kids romped. Horses pranced as they pulled carriages down paths and roads.

Late in the afternoon I returned to Union Station and climbed onto the Burlington again and rode back to Hinsdale imagining that my father was sitting in the seat across from me. When I arrived in Hinsdale, I walked three blocks to Washington Park, a place filled with endless memories of my youth. Each winter, the township flooded a ball field and turned it into an ice rink. I watched kids and adults of all ages as they sped across the ice as the temperature dipped into the teens. It was there at Washington Park that I had learned to skate. All the joyful and glorious hours I had spent with my friends, Saturdays and Sundays from morning till evening.

Sitting in the warming house on the old wooden bench carved with names and hearts and arrows, my thoughts were filled with the days we would come in from the ice with frosted fingers and blow hot breath onto our palms and go out to the ice again for another thirty or forty minutes, speeding past the girls in our seventh or eight grade classes, grabbing their caps as they screamed until we circled the rink and tossed them back again. It was on the ice at Washington Park that I dreamed of one day becoming a professional hockey player, a left winger for the

Chicago Blackhawks. I soon realized that my childhood fantasy was unlikely to come true.

In the morning, I thanked Elvie and told Ben to keep me abreast of developments and carefully tucked the photo album and the martini shaker into my duffel and called for an airport cab.

The sky over Bradford when I arrived was as gray as the preternatural winter sheet that hung over Chicago while I was there. Ha…I must have brought it back with me from the big city. I placed the photos of my father on a shelf in my closet. The martini shaker was given a prominent place on my bookcase. I thought about him doing what made him enjoy the last remnants of the day. The, "Hello, Nicholas," as I came in the door. Words spoken in a voice some might find gruff if unfamiliar with the stoic but kind man.

Sitting at my desk trying to pull myself into the present I calculated what I needed to do to catch up on my schoolwork. If I had a concern about any of it, Grayson's course was on the top of the list. I opened my biology text and flipped the pages of my notebook. "What the fuck is this?" I muttered, looking at what greeted me. Weird child-like doodling on the edge of the page. I don't doodle in class. I write frantically just trying to keep up. Confused, I went to the window and stared at the buildings and the sky. The happy, growling, bored, snarling gargoyles. The students zigzagging across campus like ants on a mission. I turned and looked at my room. Something was amiss. Something did not seem right. It had that nettling feeling you get when you put on a familiar t-shirt that doesn't seem to fit right. Funny how it is that we know every millimeter of the space we occupy and yet rarely pay attention to it.

Back to the closet again. All my shirts were jammed oddly to the side. I tried to make sense of something that made little sense. Did I do that? Possibly. Moving quickly on my way to Chicago I grabbed handfuls of clothes and stuffed them into my duffel, thoughts far off on other matters.

Grayson's class was due to start in five minutes. I snatched my book bag, sent a short text to Mona telling her I was back, and fled across campus to class. It felt good to be sitting in the lecture hall. Even felt good to see Grayson charge across the front of the room in a crest of hyperbolic energy.

Mona and I met up in Psychology, the first chance we had to see each other. Afterward, we went to my room and made up for our time apart. Lying in bed, I told her about my trip to Chicago and the Art Institute. My visit to the folk-art collection and how I was now one of its biggest fans.

For no special reason I can think of now, I mentioned the odd feeling I had that someone had been in my room. The jumbled shirts in my closet. The scribbled marks in my biology notebook.

Mona sat up. "You don't think Lunz was in here, do you?"

"I don't know."

"I heard he's been floating around the dorm again."

"The thought did occur," I said. "I told the SOB I knew he had a master key and that he better stay out of my room. And, of course, he probably knew I was away. He knows everything that happens on campus. I brought my manuscript with me thinking I might have a minute or two to add a few words but I barely had any time at all."

"It's possible he was in here and that he wanted you to know it. Why else would he write in your notebook? I think this is all part of Lunz's schtick. It's a power thing, a control thing. That's what I think," Mona said.

"It had to be Lunz," I said. "It would have been easy for Berman to get in, but I can't picture him doing it. The guy's afraid of his own shadow. I agree, it must have been Lunz. He's paranoid. He thinks people are ratting on him to the FBI." I told Mona about my encounter with him before I left for Chicago, careful not to mention the bumper sticker he waved in my face. "He was ecstatic about getting their NPP candidate elected to Congress, totally scorched about it. It was sickening to watch him. Now he's got another campaign he'll be working on soon. Something about a special election for a goon up in Wyoming."

22

Winter winds chilled the air. The days grew evermore short as the hemisphere tilted away from the sun. Slowly, slowly, like the persistent crawl of a caterpillar to the underside of a leaf.

I received a call from Ben telling me the house sold almost as soon as it was placed on the market. It bagged over a million dollars. I had no idea what I would do with that many ducats. Not to mention the mountain of wealth that came from what my father had stuffed into savings and stocks throughout his life. His acumen with money allowed him to generate a sizeable portfolio and, being the frugal man he was, little was spent on anything of frivolity. No expensive cruises. No getaways in the sun or cabins in the mountains. What I would do with that much money, I had no idea.

Need I say that Krause Lunz appeared at my door not long after Mona left? "Heard you went back to Chicago. Sorry to hear about Pop," he said, in a voice devoid of sympathy as he stepped in the room. He quickly slid into his usual philippics. "Missed some classes, huh? Well, fear not. Missing class here at the Brad isn't something to worry about. I'm proof of that. You can almost predict what will come out of Tangsley's mouth, so you can write that one off. And any bozo can flash through the list of novels they want you to read in English Lit. As for biology, don't know squat about what that entails. Never bothered to sign up for, for you know, for that junk. Howie Berman, he's a bio major, pre-med. All the kikes, they all want to go to medical school." He rubbed his thumb and fingertips together to signify money. "They all want to be doctors…it's where the bucks are. That's Berman, for sure. Pre-med. Don't know about Jennifer Rubinstein. Probably her as well. She seems like the kind of bagel who would go to medical school. In fact, pretty certain I saw a bunch of biology and chemistry books once when I was in the room Holly and Rubinstein share. Rubinstein's books no doubt. You can be sure Holly Clarke has no plans to be a doctor."

"I hope you got rid of that revolting bumper sticker," I said.

Lunz shrugged, which told me he hadn't.

"And while we're at it, someone was in my room while I was gone. You weren't in here snooping around, were you? I warned you what would happen if you ever tried to—"

"Cut it out, Schefield. What the hell would I want in here? Go ask Berman. He's the guy in charge of the dorm."

"Fuck Berman," I said. "Someone was in here. I can prove it." I reached for my biology notebook.

Lunz waved off the comment. "I've got more important things to do than poke around in dorm rooms. I'm heading off to Wyoming to work on the campaign of an NPP flop up there. Charlie Smith but goes by the name Chubby…Chubby Smith. How's *that* for a goddamn name…Chubby! All these hicks have names like that. Chubby!"

"Are they the best you can find?"

"No worse than the hambones already in Congress," Lunz replied. "The reason is simple. The problem is not the morons who are getting elected. The problem is the morons who are electing them. So, you see, we don't really give a shit who wants to run on the NPP ticket. We're a hell of a damn good EEOC employer, we are. And this country is saturated with white folks who want to step up to do their patriotic duty. They want to prevent the country from going down a rat hole before it's too late. *Achtung!*" He threw his shoulders back and snapped his heels and held his arm out. "Don't think the great old U. S. of A. has been run by a bunch of choirboys all these years. It's well documented that Prescot Bush, grandaddy of George W, who as we know was never actually elected. The Supremes made him president when the garbage over the hanging chads happened in Florida. *Más corrupción, amigo!* But I digress…where was I? Oh, yes, Prescott was a director of Union Banking Corporation, an investment firm that was financing Hitler's move to power, among other things, in the nineteen-thirties. This is well known. It's ready to be found by anyone looking for it. The Dulles bros, too—John Foster and Allen. War criminals of the worst kind. And what do we do with people like that? Throw them in jail? Fuck no! We name an airport after them, Dulles International in DC. Makes you want to barf."

These might have been the only true words to dribble from his mouth during the many exhausting hours he babbled and pontificated.

Lunz continued. "And then we name an airport after Reagan. One of the most devious pricks to park his ass in the Oval Office. Should have been impeached for the Iran-Contra farce. I'm no fan of Clinton, that's for *damn* sure, but he was impeached for doing nothing but getting his dick wet," Lunz laughed long and hard. "But, of course, everyone loved Reagan. You know, cowboy. What's more American than that? Actor…if you want to call making movies with a chimpanzee acting. A wife as stiff and cold as a mannequin."

"So why are all your candidates in political backwaters somewhere?"

"Not so. We're grooming people all over the place. Got a homegrown guy right there in Chicago. Yep, in your place, Chicago. And when he gets elected, dear old Richard M. Daley is gonna fart in his grave."

"Got a long way to go before you folks get control of Congress."

"Already said we don't need to get full control of Congress. Listen up, dude. All movements start slow. You watch, two years from now, four at the most, we'll have a nice flock of NPP hardliners in the House. Might even tuck one into the Senate as well. We're working on it. Moving along fine, if you need to know."

"Doesn't matter, you still need a joker to run the whole thing, don't you? A Mussolini of some kind, right? At least that's what I remember from the Gospel According to Krause Wilhelm Lunz."

"One thing at a time. See, that's why organizations like the NPP need people like me…why Crocket wants so desperately for me to join his staff in Washington. They need someone who can see the future. Someone who can manage the whole shebang. Otherwise, before you know it the wheels start coming off the cart. Crockett knows that. He might be a hick but he's not stupid. He knows the organization needs to be managed. If you don't, you end up with a bunch of goons like what's her name, the one from Georgia, you know, the dykie one…dyke or trans, no question about it. You can bet she's got a pecker tucked away down in those drawers of hers. Christ, I wouldn't fuck that with your dick," he said in a wild outburst. "Or that Annie Oakley chick from the boonies out west. Well, neither of them has a clue what they're doing. They don't know shit about anything. Trust me, that's not good for their movement, whatever the hell it is they're trying to do. They're both cut out of the same mold. Both toking away on a great big ego-hookah. Puff, puff, puff. Getting higher and higher and not accomplishing a goddamn thing! Throwing biscuits to the legion of reporters who snuggle up behind them. That won't happen to us. We know how to control the media. Especially the lefties on cable. Just make sure you burp them now and then and give them plenty of fingerpaint to play with to keep their mind off the real issues. Corporate media doesn't want to deal with issues. Issues are boring and Americans have the attention span of a worm."

"Still think you got a long way to go."

"*Oy vey!*" Lunz said impatiently. "Forget that shit. What I'm here to tell you is that we've got a rally coming up right here at wonderful Bradford University. People from our group, students, all kinds of NPP. You might not know it but there's a pretty big bunch of NPP right here at the school. They'll be there. And a lot of others from outside, too.

"You can't be serious."

"Serious as hell. All the liberal chowderheads here at the Brad are in for a real treat. This is how you get converts. You get out there and mess with people's minds. It worked for centuries for everyone from *Jesus Christos* to dear old Adolf and even one of your heroes, MLK. And that Muhammad freak, too. Him, for sure. Look how many people he roped into his traveling road show over the centuries. Unfortunately for the rest of us he was a goddamn pro at screwing with people's heads."

Lunz paced the floor as if waiting for me to respond. "You're planning to bring a pack of neos and supremacists to campus," I finally said. "Is that it?" It was clear from the look on his face this was not some notion that floated into his head to get a rise out of me. "I don't think you're allowed to spread your rot all over campus."

"They can't stop us. And by the way, what I'm talking about is our *opinions*...not rot. It's our beliefs. Our convictions. Be clear on that."

"All a bunch of *rot* to me—"

"Don't really need your approval, señor Schefield, if you need to know."

"And you think the school will let you do this, that they're going to—"

"They have no choice. They *have* to. This is an institution of higher education, a place of enlightenment, or so they like to pretend, where opinions and beliefs can exist without reproach. Or have you failed to grasp that in your brief tenure here at the Brad? But I understand, once you start drinking the Kool-Aid the high priests here at the Brad serve up it's damn hard to have an original thought at all."

"And what makes you think the school will give you a permit?"

"Already have. There is not a freaking thing anyone can do now. It's all set. It'll happen soon enough."

"Someone's going to get hurt. You know that, don't you, Lunz?"

"Not because of us. The rally is going to be peaceful. It's an NPP recruitment event, nothing more."

"Bullshit! That's total bullshit! It will end up getting bloody. What kind of idiot are you, Lunz?"

"If there are people who can't handle what we're doing, what we're saying, they shouldn't come to the rally. They should stay away. Simple as that."

"It's not that simple at all. Look what happened at Charlottesville."

A long persistent silence. Lunz looked at his watch and got up and walked to the door. "Sorry to hear about your Pop," he said as he left.

23

The semester ended. Mona and I came away with a string of As. I was glad to be done. Mona departed for Washington. With nowhere to call home, I stayed at Bradford. Most of the school remained open: the cafeteria, the Union, the library. And there was always the option of going to one of the simple restaurants in Huntington Wells.

After the holidays I would go to Washington for a few days to visit Mona and her family. I was not as fear-struck at the thought of that as I had been the first time I met them. We will have a "swell time", Mona declared with grandeur, snatching a phrase from *The Sun Also Rises* that she had read as part of her English class. We would get a personalized tour of the National Gallery of Art by her mother, and a visit to the Department of Justice with her father, which Mona said is really very interesting.

I had almost a full month of unfettered time to spend on my novel. I made good progress. Did I like what I wrote? I detested every word of it but I kept slogging away as best I could.

Winter settled on campus in all its dubious glory. Cold and sleepy-dark some days. Refulgently brilliant others. Mornings, I went for a run through the sleepy streets of Huntington Wells and out into the nearby countryside, wrapped to the gills in a windbreaker, ski mask, scarf, and hands and fingers tight in gloves. By the time I arrived at my destination my lungs burned from the cold clean air. Then, upon returning to campus, I had coffee or tea in my room or went to the Union for a pastry or a bagel. In the stillness of the near-deserted campus I set a goal of six hundred good words and would try for a thousand were it not for the days when the muse, like an impish fickle cat, refused to grant a single syllable worthy of the page. If nothing else, I realized how grueling writing could be. I broke the tedium with frequent calls to Mona. As best I could tell or cared to know, Lunz had left campus. His door remained closed. I heard nary a peep from inside.

January 3. I made my way to Washington to see Mona. Her parents had a wonderful house impeccably decorated by Mona's mother. We went through every section of the National Gallery of Art, the highlight being the American Folk Gallery that her mother curated. I told her about my visit to the Art Institute of Chicago and how I had become an immediate fan of the work. She gave me a vast education about a genre of art I had previously regarded as simplistic and almost meaningless.

We went to museums of all kinds. The Holocaust Museum. The Vietnam War Memorial. Chilling displays of how we, the most evolved creature on the planet, destroy ourselves in the name of greed and hate, in the fear that political systems will spill over onto our shores. Wandering through the bustling metropolis, we took a tour of the Capital and the White House and stopped at cafés for coffee or at a deli for a Reuben or pastrami sandwich as temperatures dug into the teens. It was there, sitting with a cup of coffee on a cold winter day, that I told Mona of my plans to pack my schedule in the spring semester with as many writing courses as I could. But deep inside, I had an urge to give up school altogether and find that small, quiet island in the Caribbean where I could spend all my time writing. I was tempted to tell Mona this but, *comme ci comme ça*, I knew I could never bring myself to be away from her. My heart fluttered every time I looked at her. She had become an opioid I could not resist. On those days when both of Mona's parents were at work, we snuck off to her room for a hot rendezvous. Life was good!

Topping off the week, we went to a hockey game between the Washington Capitals and the Chicago Blackhawks. What incredible fun. A chance to see a trinity of legendary hockey players on the ice at once: Alex Ovechkin, Jonathan Toews, and Patrick Kane. The Blackhawks won in a shootout.

I returned to Bradford. Mona would be back in a couple of days. The spring semester would start in mid-January. I flew to Boston and boarded a bus for New Hampshire. The campus was already filling with students. I went to the dorm and dropped my duffel on the floor and sat for a moment in the chair and thought about the new semester. My desires to be a doctor or a diplomat were gone once and for all. I would not miss any of it. Not even the days when I watched the near comic routine of Grayson as he cavorted across the front of the room. It had become painfully evident that Krebs cycles and molecular biology were not my cup of tea. I did, however, manage to miraculously plug through the course with an A after a painful week of cramming every factoid of the subject into my brain, the details of which to this day I barely recall.

I went to the window. A bulging sky predicted soon-to-arrive heavy snow. I had seen this a thousand times in Chicago before it was about to deposit a layer of thick white powder that rendered the city a place of angelic beauty until the reality of it turned the act of walking and driving into a deadly task. I stared at the buildings, the ever-present gargoyles that were about to be capped in white berets. I felt good from my week visiting Mona and her parents and yet I knew that my life would return to where it had left off. Endless tormenting days listening to Lunz. On my way back to Bradford, I prepared myself for his perpetual assaults. I knew he was probably back on campus and knew that it would be just a matter of time before he would saunter down the hall and swagger into my room. I closed the door and turned out the lights.

Having slept well during the night, I got up early, made a cup of coffee, tried to turn my attention to my novel, gave up, and started unpacking my duffel as Lunz paraded into the room with all the pizzazz of a guest on a late-night talk show.

"Don't you ever knock?" I said, removing clothes from the bag.

In his hand was a book that he rudely deposited on my desk. "There she is. Take a gander."

I glanced abstractly at what he had defiled my workspace with. A bound paperback of *Unser Kampf*. Red cover with a white circle and black NPP letters inside. Along the bottom, the words A Manifesto for America by Krause Wilhelm Lunz were displayed in scripted Gothic letters exactly as on the manuscript he had previously delivered to me.

"Take a gander," Lunz repeated boldly. "*Published.* A damn beauty if I do say so myself. A raving beauty! And you, my good man, get a first-edition copy. Hot off the press. Ink ain't even dry yet." Lunz's eyes filled with savoir delight. "Just think, someday that book there will be as valuable as an original copy of *Mein Kampf.* And you, Schefield, have the privilege of getting one of the very first copies!"

"How many times are you going to thrust this crap at me, Lunz?"

"Jesus…how ungrateful! Here I am delivering the best Christmas present you'll ever get," Lunz said, then added, "Notice I did not say the best Hanukkah present. Sorry, should have said Holiday present…right?"

"Screw you, Lunz. Do you really believe people are going to read that shit? Do you?"

"The publisher is pumping out copies like linked sausages. Just wait, you'll see. What do you think? Cover is damn hot, huh?"

"Looks dreadful. Pretty easy to tell from that the kind of bilge you've packed inside."

"We already sold more than two thousand copies the first day out. Get that, two thousand damn copies! And you thought no one would read it. Well, think again. The words in that little gem will speak volumes to every cretin in this country. To all the buffoons looking for a way to escape from the pulverizing blasphemy they've been fed, the crap they've had to suffer through their whole life. Read it, read it! You'll see," he said as he sank down in the chair and dropped his feet onto the ottoman.

I shoved the book to the edge of my desk.

"All right," Lunz said. "So how was the vacation? Back to Chicago? Oh, forgot…probably not much reason to go there now, huh?" He let out a slow groan as if hunting for a reason to stay longer. "Aaah, I'm finishing up this semester. Being paroled from the goddamn Bradford Penal Institution."

"With a degree?"

"Of course, Schefield, of course. See, I'm living proof that dumps like Bradford are totally fraudulent. Won't be long before I sail out of here *Suma Cum Laude* with a perfect 4.0."

"With a major in what? You never did tell me. PE, I suppose."

"Ha, ha, ha, funny, funny," Lunz said.

"Well?"

"German…if you need so desperately to know."

"Sounds a lot like PE to me. I'm sure any clown could pull off a degree in German."

"Shows how little you know. A degree in German is real sophisticated shit. One of the toughest majors at the Brad. Had to read scores of books in German, real deep stuff. I'm damn near fluent in it now. Could have written *Unser Kampf*, the whole goddamn thing, in German. Every bloody word."

"Wonderful."

"I never told you, but I spent most of my sophomore year in Germany. Yeah, I could have written *Unser Kampf* in German but there's not a single schlub in this country who would have been able to read it." He leaned back and slipped down in the chair. "Okay, enough of that shit. The real news of the day is that everything is moving along great with the special election of Chubby Smith. I spent a couple of weeks up in Wyoming working on his campaign. Came away with a helluva nice cowboy hat, a black one. Well, Chubby is going to sail through the election just like old Horace Crockett did." Lunz puffed up proudly. "Two elections, two wins."

"I'm supposed to be impressed?"

"Speaking of Crockett, I also stopped by for a few days

down in DC and helped him get his staff together. And guess what? Those two troublemakers—the Annie Oakley chick from out west and the butchy one from Georgia—they came by to pay their respects to Horace. I guess they don't have much to do but fart around in their offices and throw dog biscuits to reporters. Anyway, they stopped by to welcome Horace to the fold. Like we really need those dorks…yeah, right! I told Crockett to keep his distance. They'd be nitro to our movement, to the NPP. He got the point, he knows. He may look like a hick with that dumb ass comb over of his but the guy is smarter than you might think. Those country lawyers can snooker you right out of your skivvies if you're not careful."

"Sounds to me like that hand cart of yours is racing straight on down to hell."

"See, Schefield, you joke about it but some real bad shit is going to happen in this country…sooner rather than later. And once the ball gets rolling there's no stopping it. That's why Prescott Bush and those two wily Dulles bros were always greasing dear old Adolph. They thought he was a joke, a gasbag who liked to get up and scream about how he would get Germany back in shape. They thought they could make bundles of money off the guy. And truth is, they did. If you want to make it rich, forget the Board of Trade and Wall Street crap. Go straight for the war machinery stuff. Raytheon, General Electric, companies like that. Tie up with Silicon Valley. For us it will be simple: get control of Congress, get a Mussolini or a Hitler in the Oval Office, someone who cares about power, not ego. Pass laws to scrub out the libraries. Fix the Constitution once and for all, maybe get rid of it once and for all. Stop the flood of bad actors coming in from Central America and the droves of Muslims coming in from everywhere. The Chinese, the Vietnamese, the Indians and all the other countries. I mean, go figure, the population of China and India are both over a billion, more like a billion and a half each. No damn wonder they want to dump a shitload of people on us. So what? We'll make sure people of a certain kind *cannot* serve in Congress. Make sure only *true* Americans can serve. Once we do that the rest will be a snap. Herr Goering explained it perfectly at Nuremberg after the war. He said it's easy to bring the people to do the bidding of a leader. Tell them they're being attacked and accuse the peacemakers of being unpatriotic. Lunz watched my reaction. "I can tell you don't believe it."

"Tall order, Lunz. Anyway, how do you plan to get control of the country now that Agent Orange is in charge?"

"Trump?"

"Yes, Trump. Who else? He sort of short-circuits your plans, it seems."

"We're not worried. He's absolutely perfect for us because he'll take the country apart piece by piece. Look at all the clucks he put in charge of running the government. Mark my word— bad news for the country, good news for the NPP. On top of it, Netanyahu has Trump in his pocket. Israel is headed for war with Iran. It's unavoidable. When that happens, Israel will come crying to Trump; he'll have no option but to join forces with them. Then you've got Israel and the US fighting Iran. Who is Iran's biggest ally? Russia. Get the picture? Damn near World War Three. Wait until Iran puts one of our aircraft carriers with five thousand sailors down on the bottom of the Gulf of Oman or the Persian Gulf. Congress will freak. The country will freak. Fact is, the people who flocked to Trump's rallies loved listening to him because he pontificated like ole' Adolph did. He's trying to be a dictator now and who knows, he might succeed. But he has the attention span of a fruit fly. Watch the guy. He leaps from one topic to another. All he wants to do is see his fat face on *Fox and Friends*. He's like Narcissus who couldn't stop staring at his reflection in the water. It became a curse because he couldn't tear himself away. So, you see, in the end Trump's ego will destroy him if his mental decline doesn't get to him first. He's slipping quickly into Alzheimer's, frontotemporal dementia maybe. But it will be his ego that finally destroys him. His second term will be worse than the first. Far worse. So bad, in fact, that the country will be waiting desperately for someone, anyone, to lead. The people around him know it. They're preparing for it, and none of them have any idea of what they're gonna do when the final curtain comes down. There will be a massive power struggle. It will turn into a chaotic mess. That's when the NPP will step in. Horace Crockett knows this. He said he can see it starting already."

"Probably…I don't know. Then you've still got to contend with the radical organizations like the Oath Keepers, the Proud Boys, the Three Percenters, yada, yada. They're going to be waiting in the wings."

"That bunch?" Lunz flashed the middle finger. "They're done. All a bunch of hapless losers. Christ, they could screw up a one-car parade. I could give you a whole lecture on how to succeed and how they all fumbled the ball from the get-go. German might be my major but I know a hell of a lot about history, world history. And I don't mean the flavor Tangsley or anyone else serves up here at Bradford. And political science too. I've forgotten more about that crap than the so-called profs here will ever know. I've learned a hell of a lot about how to control people. One of the few good things I gleaned from Shrink 1 and Shrink

2. Think of me as Joseph Goebbels, Hitler's propaganda jock. The only one of the pack who had half a brain. It's kind of like that joke about the mafia: it's made up of twelve wops named Vito and a guy named Morris who can count." Lunz slapped his hand on his leg and bent over in laughter.

"Look what happened to Goebbels."

"I know, I know. But the problem wasn't Goebbels. It was Adolph. If Goebbels could have kept the Kraut in line, everything would have been fine."

"So what, who cares? Fuck all this Nostradamus garbage. What I want to know is what's going on with that rally of yours?"

"It's coming, it's coming."

"You need to cancel it before it's too late."

"Not on your life. Do you know how many NPP we have at the school already?"

"Too many."

"You see, even schools like this, even schools like the Brad, as pinko as it is, has a teeny-tiny core of right-wingers. They go by names like Young Republicans. Stupid names like that. Harvard, Yale, all the blue-blood places have similar groups. Bunch of uninformed sponge heads who don't know shit about anything and are always spouting off about what they learned from their parents. The school loves having them here because they come from families with deep pockets...you know, the fucking legacy thing. The kids merely scam their way through a degree, get drunk in the dorms and frat houses, and do a rain dance to the almighty greenback until it's time to get their rich fannies out of here and into law school or off to Harvard for an MBA. They're easy pickins' for us because most of them feel entitled and they hate their parents with a passion. This is the way they screw their parents;

they know it'll drive mommy and daddy nuts."

I wondered if Lunz realized what he said. I thought about his parents whom he seemed to despise so bitterly. Was the NPP a grief war he was waging against them?

"Just wait, we'll pick up a lot of students once they hear what the NPP is all about. They're all looking for a way to escape from the mental dungeons their parents locked them in. There are a lot of students who want to scrub themselves clean of the socialist garbage that comes out of schools like dear old Bradford University. They're sick of the woke stuff. They're sick of being treated like children and being told what to believe and what not to believe. You pointy-headed liberals built a proverbial house of cards, one card after another, unaware of how shaky and wobbly the whole thing is. Falling apart under the weight."

A glorious week with Mona and now back to the Lunz torture chamber again as if I were caught in an eternal time warp I could not escape from.

"Isn't there anyone else here at Bradford you can find to puke this out to, Lunz? You know, I've listened to your bullshit for months now, and here's what I think. I think you're a totally fucked up wreck. Full of shit all the way to the eyeballs. I watched you try to bait me. Despite what you think, I am *not* an idiot. You are one sorry son-of-a-bitch. I don't know if you believe all the shit you tell me. The crap that's in that…whatever it's called." I waved my hand at the copy of *Unser Kampf* on my desk.

Lunz was unexpectedly still.

"You come in here and tell me how you're planning a fascist takeover of the country. Maybe it's true, maybe you will. Well, the very thought of it disgusts me. I never said America is perfect. For Christ's sake, show me a country that is. And while we're at it, you seem to have forgotten, or *ignored*, the fact that all those glorious fascist regimes you so proudly boast of self-destructed, sooner or later they all go down from their own inertia. Never talk much about that, do you? You treat me like an idiot, insult me. I know you come in here every day trying to see how many buttons you can push. Pretty sick. I see the look on your face when you do. The ways you rag on about all the people you hate. Ranting perpetually about Jews and Blacks and Latinos and Muslims and Asians. How many of those people have done anything to screw up your life? And the way you eternally bitch about your parents. Guess what, Lunz, we don't get to choose our parents, so suck it up buttercup. And all the crude and offensive stuff you said about Holly Clarke and Jennifer Rubinstein…the dirty innuendos about Mona. The problem with you is that you hate the whole world. God almighty, you can't even find anything good to say about your own damn group, the NPP—not that I think there is much good to say about them. Every millimeter of your body is riddled with hatred through and through." Lunz watched in utter silence. The second I stopped talking, a sense of calm passed through me as if I was cleansed of everything that had been building in me for months. As if I had been to confession. As though my soul had been rid of the anger I harbored from all the hours I had tolerated Lunz.

Lunz stared blankly across the room and got up and left.

24

It snowed from morning till night the next day. I had an early class. Mona had two in the morning and one in the afternoon. I worked on my novel as much as possible. My writing professor had the determination of a mob don. It was clear that if she could not turn us into writers, she would at least give us a taste of what good writing entailed. Besides countless writing assignments, she assailed us with a long list of books, novellas, and short stories to read. Books we could buzz through with little effort. All of which had the intended effect: *Cannery Row*, *The Actual*, *The Torrents of Spring*, dozens more. All humbling experiences to a fledgling writer. I would at times re-read entire passages by Saul Bellow in search of one clumsy sentence—just one. It did not exist. And then I would go back and read the perfectly crafted pages from one of Patrick Modiano's books.

The snow on the window ledge brought thoughts of my fantasy island in the Caribbean and the cabin cruiser I would set to the water each day after a morning of writing. The sun and the sea mist. How fun it was to dream such. I picked up the pages of my novel and read what I had written to that point. I knew more than ever that it was hopelessly bad but I would keep plugging along nonetheless. Perhaps it would get better. Or perhaps I could fix it the way you mend a broken picket fence, patch it up and try to make it work. It was a nice thought. If nothing else, the character of Krause Lunz was easily recognized by anyone who knew him. *Fine*, I thought. *What's it matter? He's not likely to see it and even if he did, why should I care?*

In the afternoon while sitting in Ponzo's restaurant with Mona and Holly Clarke and Jennifer Rubinstein. I told them about the rally Lunz was planning.

Jennifer said she had heard about it from Howie Berman. "He comes around a lot and bugs the crap out of me. He said Lunz is planning to import a bunch of neos, neo-Nazis and white supremacists. That he's planning to bring a slew of them in for the rally."

"Oh God, no! This is terrible," Mona said. "Doesn't he know what will happen? Someone will get hurt. Doesn't he know?"

"I tried to tell him," I said. "He claimed they have a permit from the school. The date is set. I don't know…maybe we should go away that day."

"Not me! No way! I'll be there," Mona said. "I want to hear, I want to see, everything that goes on. All the BS propaganda that the NPP will be peddling. I want to hear every word of it."

If Mona was going to the rally, I would be there. The whole thing could explode into a massive Vesuvius of hate and violence.

I said, "In the beginning I was never quite sure whether to believe what Lunz said. I guess I pretended he was just pumping this stuff out because…because that's the kind of loser he is. I cut him a lot of slack tricking myself into thinking it was all a big bluff on his part. But now I know he's serious. The first time it really clicked was when they got their NPP candidate elected to Congress. Horace Crockett down in Alabama. Then I knew it was no joke. Then I knew there was trouble ahead. It scared the hell out of me. He told me the NPP is well organized but they need a leader. Someone to take control of the movement. In a weird way, I've wondered if he's planning to move in and fill the void himself. That's scary…damn scary. He certainly has the hutzpah to do it."

"We have to fight hatred," Mona said. "We have to. Always, always, always. It's the only way to defeat it. If we give up, Lunz and the NPP and his collection of misfits will win. This is a fight for democracy. Remember what it says on the masthead of *The Washington Post*: Democracy Dies In Darkness. I will never quit fighting. I'll never let people like Lunz or groups like the NPP spread their hatred. If I have an ounce of strength left in me, I will do everything I can to prevent it."

Holly asked when the rally was scheduled.

"Sometime this semester. I'm not sure when," I said.

"Berman must know," Jennifer said. "He's tight with Lunz. The next time he comes by I'll see what I can find out. I agree with Mona. We need to be at the rally. We need to have tons of people there to dilute the effect of the NPP. *Lots*. Make it look like their movement is trivial, that it can be stopped, that it's nothing at all."

We ordered pizza and stayed at the restaurant until late and tried to put aside our thoughts about Lunz and the NPP and turned our attention to our classes for the new semester. Music by Pearl Jam, Incubus, and Arctic Monkeys filled the room. I was glad to be away from the dorm and spend time with Mona and Jennifer and Holly.

Walking back through campus Mona and I stopped at the Union as a student attached a flyer on the wall. There was the answer to our question. It advertised an upcoming event in February.

Join The National Peoples Party – The NPP – On the Quadrangle February 3rd. Meet Congressman Horace Crockett and Others from the NPP

We stared at the wall. What Lunz boasted of was now certain to happen. Walking silently across campus, we settled onto a bench. I looked up at a grape evening sky. At the multitude of gargoyles that no longer made me smile, that no longer made me feel safe. Cold stone witnesses to what would happen on February 3rd. I could feel the inner gloom that filled Mona, eyes drawn onto the ground.

"Why does stuff like this happen?" she said softly. "What is it about this country that it cannot move forward, that it cannot leave the past behind? When will it recover from its old illnesses? Sometimes I feel as though it's a cancer that cannot be cured. That America is doomed to live with it forever. Always there. It makes me sick inside."

I held Mona's hand. Students moved quickly down paths returning from classes. The air blew colder by the second as we sat there.

"It makes me want to cry," Mona said in the most mournful voice.

She squeezed my palm tightly then let go and swept a tear from her eye. "Oh, *mon amour*, what will we do? What will we do?"

"We'll be ready, just as you said when we were at Ponzo's. That's what we'll do. That is all we can do."

Mona looked at the sky. "We will have a group of our own to defy the NPP," she said with new resolve. "Hundreds of people. Hundreds! No matter who Lunz brings, no matter where they come from, we will show them that evil cannot win…that it will *never* win."

Within days, more signs advertising the rally appeared throughout campus. We had barely two weeks to prepare for it. Mona laid out a strategy of how to form an NPP resistance group. Day after day she contacted her vast collection of friends, held meetings, talked about what would happen in a few weeks, begged people to spread the word. I posted signs encouraging students to show up in the quad on February 3rd. As time drew closer, I felt tension grow across campus.

I had just returned to my room when Krause Lunz burst in. I had not heard from him since the day I returned to campus after my trip to Washington. Perhaps he had at last given up on me. I looked up from the novella I was reading. Lunz had a mean sneer pinched across his face. He wasted no time bursting into a rage. "I saw the garbage you assholes are stringing around campus,"

I waited for the rest of what was about to erupt from him.

"Doesn't matter. If you folks want a confrontation, so be it," he said, slamming his fist on the door jam. "The NPP is coming to campus peacefully."

"Fat chance," I snapped. "There is no goddamn way you're going to flood the quad with the NPP and have it come off peacefully."

"So, who's the troublemaker now, Schefield? All we're planning to do is have a simple little recruitment event for the group.

174

Let people know what the NPP stands for. That and *nothing* more."

"Oh, cut the crap! That's bullshit!" I yelled. "The more trouble you make the happier you'll be. I've seen you in action for months now. You and those NPP assholes who follow around behind you. Are you going to tell the people at the rally that you're a bunch of neo-Nazis, that you're white supremacists? Are you? Hell no, of course not! You're not about to do that. Who the hell are you trying to kid?"

"For Christ's sake, Mister Schefield, spare me your gloomy prognostications! You're expecting trouble and nothing has happened yet," Lunz howled, his face cherry red.

"There is going to be trouble, and *you* know it."

"We have every right in the world to gather, it's called freedom to assemble. That's why the school made no effort to stop us. Get off your ass and read the Constitution. That holy, or should I say unholy, pack of so-called laws. The First Amendment to the Constitution. The very first amendment. *Numero uno*. 'Congress shall make no law respecting an establishment of religion, or prohibiting the free exercise thereof; or abridging the freedom of speech, or of the press; or the right of the people peaceably to assemble, and to petition the government for redress of grievances. That says it all. Freedom of speech. Peaceable assembly. Go read it, buster!"

"Screw you. Besides, I thought you hated the Constitution."

"We use whatever is available to us. Just like you do. Have you failed to realize that your plans to destroy our assembly are guaranteed by the very same Constitution? But of course you pinkos believe you're entitled, believe that you're special. Go ahead, slap your fucking signs all over campus. Fill them with lies about the NPP. We will be in the quad on February 3rd no matter what. And there is not a *goddamn thing* you can do to stop us." Lunz spun and tore out of the room.

I didn't know if Lunz was attempting to scare us into short-circuiting our plans or whether he was maniacally out of control. It did not matter because either way his anger fueled my desire to stand up to the NPP at all costs. I tried to imagine what February 3rd would be like. My father was not a person given to offering advice. I could count the times he had done that on the fingers of one hand, though I remembered him once telling me that there are very few things in life we can actually change once momentum takes over, but it does not mean we should just quit and give up. The more difficult the problem, the more important it is to try harder. I suppose this was the first time I realized what he meant.

And of course, there was Mona—life's poster child for determination when it came to matters like this. More than anything, she was the core of my inspiration.

I sat in my room filled with dread, my body tight as a piano string. Each day was getting worse. I left the dorm and went to the library and located an empty reading room, a place where the afternoon sun sprinkled kind and happy rays through the stained-glass windows. Sitting in a chair, I folded my arms on the table and rested my head on them. I thought about my brief six months at Bradford. What a rocky journey it had been. The joyful days and nights with Mona. The misery of dealing with the sewage that oozed from Lunz almost daily. Thoughts of whether coming to Bradford had been a good idea after all. I could have stayed in Chicago. Could have gone to any of the good universities there— Northwestern, The University of Chicago, DePaul. But then, I would never have met Mona. What a pitiful thought! Or I suppose I could throw in the towel once and for all and find the tiny island I fantasized about. I knew, of course, I would not do that, knew I could never leave Mona.

25

We continued to organize. Our numbers grew each day. Mona estimated at least six hundred students were firmly committed to be on the quadrangle when the NPP arrived. The energy she harnessed permeated through every corner of the campus. She was determined to make sure that the NPP were outmatched and that Lunz's rally was trivial and meaningless. When not in her room studying or in class she was drumming up as many people as possible to be present on the quadrangle. I continued to post signs on bulletin boards urging students to attend in the hopes of mitigating the message of the NPP. The momentum was growing by the hour.

Lunz made no visits to my room. When I walked down the hall his door was invariably cracked two inches as always. He was engaged in fiery conversations on his phone. A premonition of what was to come, a premonition that said fate might not be kind to us.

Time dribbled by.

The air outside on the eve of the rally dipped into the forties. A chalky sky hid whatever warmth the sun had promised for the day. The NPP was due on campus at two o'clock the next afternoon. We spent the night in Mona's room in episodes of fitful sleep. In the morning, we went to the Union for coffee. My thoughts sullen and dark, I struggled to find a smile. Students stopped and talked to Mona. She gave everyone the same advice: show up and keep a cool head. She did not want a violent confrontation with the NPP. She had no idea how many of Lunz's group would be there. All she cared about was that we were present in numbers to minimize his message. We returned to the dorm as thin clouds floated across a pallid blue sky. The day seemed no different than any other for early February.

We went to our morning classes. I barely remembered a word of what was said, not even sure I took notes. When we returned to the dorm, Lunz's door was closed. It could be said with some certainty that he was not inside. In all likelihood, off campus escorting Horace Crockett to the school.

Time ticked. Mona became quiet in a way I had never seen before. Her face bore a look of fear. She hardly talked, tried to relax, read a little, moved about the room, sat down, walked to the window, gave long empty stares at the quadrangle, came back, sat down. As noon approached, I pulled a bag of chips from my backpack. She ate a few, checked her watch, checked for texts, and said almost nothing.

An hour passed. "All right…we go."

We put on our coats and walked across campus. Mona squeezed my hand tightly. Students were already starting to file into the quadrangle. My nerves tight as a plumb line, as if waiting for the executioner to say: "The time has come," as he escorted us to the gallows.

Looking around, it was evident Mona's hard work had paid off. Students came in from all parts of the campus, from dorms, classrooms, from off-campus housing, fraternities and sororities.

Students watched from windows around the quadrangle. It had to be true that many of the classes were sparsely attended. Someone had cued the news media into what was about to happen. A half-dozen national news organizations set up shop. Cameramen and reporters milled through the crowd talking to students. I had no idea who told them about the event. Lunz, no doubt—hoping to capitalize on the quick and easy publicity. Or perhaps the mere appearance of a US Congressman, one as controversial as Horace Crockett, was enough to generate a visit from the media. Regardless, the whole affair would be recorded and might make it onto the evening news—for better or for worse.

A reporter came up to Mona, having heard she had organized groups of students. "What are your intentions for being here today?" the reporter asked.

"We want to hear what the NPP will say. To see once and for all what they believe in. Let there be no mistake, the NPP does not support the values of this country."

"It's said they have a large group of neo-Nazis and white supremacists. Is that true?"

"I don't know who will be here. I am here to see what they have to say," Mona said again.

"Do you expect a confrontation?"

"No. Absolutely not! We are here to make a strong showing on campus. I am familiar with many of the students who are here and I can tell you they do not hold to the beliefs of the NPP. The NPP espouses tyrannical ideas that are out of line with the spirit of democracy in America," Mona calmly and pointedly said.

"They already have one member of their party elected to Congress. Horace Crockett from Alabama. We were told he will be here today. Do you think the NPP is gaining a following among Americans? Does it worry you?"

"Of course it worries me," Mona replied. "That's precisely why we are here. To hear what they say."

At that point, people began to gather on the edge of campus. The reporter signaled for her crew to get over to them quickly.

At exactly two o'clock, as precisely as the moment a train pulls into a railroad station in Rome, the NPP led by Krause Lunz filed into the quadrangle like Hitler's goose-stepping gang marching through the streets of Munich. There was no confusion about who they were. All wore brown shirts and brown pants and red armbands with a white circle and large black NPP letters blazoned in the middle like the swastika brand of Nazi Germany. A drummer tapped a beat to the slamming of boots on the ground. The NPP came in unison to the heart of the quadrangle. Lunz held his hand up; the NPP stopped. Next to Lunz was a man I had no trouble recognizing. Horace Crockett. Though I had never met or seen him I was certain it was Crockett from the many descriptions Lunz had provided—as true-to-form in the flesh as in Lunz's words. A man behind them held a bullhorn. The quadrangle was rimmed by a swath of campus police and a complement of police from Huntington Wells and neighboring villages. Far too few in my opinion.

We stood at the forefront of the student group barely twenty feet from where Lunz and the NPP halted in rank. Lunz's eyes landed briefly on mine. He delivered a short grizzly smile. I made a crude estimate of the number of NPP—possibly two hundred. Could have been more. I turned and looked at the students packed in behind me. It was hard to calculate from where I stood. My best guess predicted at least five to six hundred. More continued to seep into the quadrangle from all portals. I was surprised at the ages of the NPP members. For some reason I had envisioned a much older group—people in their thirties, maybe forties, older even. But it was clear that many were young. Were they students? Some, no doubt. Others, certainly not. The distribution clearly favored males, but by no means exclusively so.

With no waste of time, Lunz grabbed the bullhorn and thanked the students for a strong showing. "Welcome one and all on this lovely day here at Bradford University. The New Hampshire weather has been kind to us. We are grateful to all of you for being here."

Applause from the NPP went up as if on script. I all but wondered when the saluting would begin, the outstretched arms.

Lunz's words echoed loud across the quadrangle. "For those who do not know me, I am Kraus Lunz, a fellow student here at wonderful Bradford University. I had the pleasure of organizing this event. The reason is simple. We want you to know what the NPP is. To understand what we stand for. To know who we are. Most of all, we want you to find out what the NPP can do for you. This is why we are here. We are a political party. That, and nothing more."

"A hate-filled political party! That and plenty more," a student shouted.

Lunz continued unfazed. With each sentence his voice rose and sank in a deep and perfected rhythm. I expected him to swing a fist and wave it in the air above him. I realized he was too savvy for that. It was clear that the days and hours he spent stumping for NPP candidates had paid off. He had learned well.

Words boomed from Lunz out into the quadrangle. "Are you sick of the useless two-party system that rules this country?

It does not matter which party you vote for, which party you are a member of. Democrat. Republican. It does not matter. They are no different. Oh, sure, they want you to believe there is a difference, but it is an illusion."

A student yelled. "Go back to hell where you came from! We know what you stand for. We know all about the evil of the NPP. Don't think we don't."

Lunz continued. "The NPP is the solution to every problem in this country. People believe that you have to be a Democrat or a Republican to get elected to Congress. That's why most people have given up on the political system in America. It's why less than half of all eligible voters cast a ballot. But we at the NPP are living proof that they are wrong. The NPP, the National Peoples Party, speaks for you. For you and for everyone in this country. We speak for you. We know what people want. We listen to people and most importantly we know what the problems of this country are and how to fix them. The problems are deep but the solutions are easy. Today, you are going to hear how America can be saved. How the NPP has the solution for every problem. In a minute you will hear from the Honorable Horace Crockett, a congressman from the great state of Alabama and a dedicated member of the NPP. He is proof that you do not need to be stuck in the past. He is proof that better choices exist."

In a voice that rose and dipped, periodically embellished with raucous cheers from the NPP, Lunz's body shook as he spoke. His shoulders swung side-to-side and up-and-down. Holding the bullhorn with one hand he thrust his other hand repeatedly in the air in outburst like the ones I had seen during his multitude of visits to my room. I could barely bring myself to watch.

He ratcheted up his fiery delivery in words that bounced off the stately buildings around the quadrangle. "Come with us to the future! Leave decayed America behind! Let it go. Move forward. Ask yourself, what has this country done for you? Stop and think. Think about it for a minute. The answer is simple…very little. Why? Because all of what could be used to make America better is being wasted. The person who can tell you this best is Congressman Crockett. And so, it is with great, great pleasure that I turn your attention to the Honorable Horace Crockett." Lunz handed the bullhorn to Crockett, tapped him fondly on the shoulder, stepped aside and wiped sweat from his brow.

Crockett waited momentarily. He looked solemnly out across the large group of students standing before him. His face displayed none of the hard-carved expressions that accompanied Lunz's oration. At that instant I realized that this simple country lawyer from the backwoods of Alabama knew what he was doing, knew how to handle a crowd. In a soft almost gentle voice, he said, "Thank you, Krause…thank you." He gazed again out at the crowd. "I want to welcome y'all to our gathering. It is a great pleasure to be here to speak to you. I am very, very humbled to have this opportunity." He paused, looked benevolently around, waited. A surreal stillness settled onto the quadrangle. "As Krause told you, I am a Congressman from Alabama, from a lovely area in the northwest corner of the state. The wonderful people of my district gave me a grand and resounding victory over a Democrat and a Republican, both of whom challenged me in the election. Everyone said I could not win. Everyone said the NPP could never win. But we did and the reason was simple. The NPP, the National Peoples Party, is the only party that adheres to the *true* spirit, the *true* tenets this country was founded on. What are these, you ask—"

"Hatred! Racism! Admit it, Crockett. That's what you believe in. Go ahead, just say so."

"Shut him up. Shut the guy up," someone from the NPP fired back. "Let the Congressman speak."

Crockett held his arm up to quiet the groups.

"Hey, Crockett, where is Der Führer? Will he be here to speak also?" Laughter broke out among the students.

"Let him speak! Let him speak!" a students cried out. "For Christ's sake, show some civility."

"Thank you," Horace Crockett said, nodding kindly. "Our beliefs at the NPP are very simple. Face it, y'all have been getting screwed for decades now. Sure, I know this is an elite university. And I know you think that your lives are fine and that you will do fine in the rest of your life. I'm sure that's what you believe. But don't forget that there are students who did not get into Bradford because they deserve to be here. They got in because…you know why they got in."

"Oh, here we go!" a student roared.

Crockett continued. "Y'all know exactly what I'm talking about. All of you do. I don't have to explain it…but I will. Programs like affirmative action. Almost everyone I see standing before me worked hard to get here. I am quite sure of that. Do y'all think it's right for students to be admitted who are *not* qualified? Do you?"

"No!" a student shouted loudly.

I was shocked at the response. I turned quickly to see where it came from. Clearly, Crockett had hit a nerve. I realized how easy it was for someone like him to enflame a crowd. He knew the ropes, the angles, the twists needed to kindle fear in people.

"I merely use affirmative action as an example of how America has lost its direction," he continued. "This country was once a meritocracy. You all know what that is. We once rewarded people for hard work, for determination, for grit, for what they achieved. But not anymore. No, not anymore."

"Tell the truth, Mr. Horace Crockett, you're a Nazi. A goddamn Nazi. Come on, just say it!" a girl in the crowd shrieked.

A skirmish suddenly broke out between a white student and a black one. Punches were thrown. People tried to pull them apart. The police plowed in and separated them. Crockett kept going. His voice gradually became louder and sharper, more direct. The tension in the quadrangle was palpable.

"People say I'm a Nazi, a white nationalist," Crockett said. "But we at the NPP merely believe that America *must* return to its origins—a country founded by *white people* on *Christian* principles. I don't have to tell you, y'all know it to be true. There is a tremendous book I want to tell you about. It was written by Krause Lunz, the person who spoke a minute ago, one of your fellow students. In it, he spells out all the problems with America and how they can be rectified. I implore you to buy it. The name of the book is *Unser Kampf*...Our Struggle. Krause lays out in simple, beautiful terms what needs to be done to solve America's problems. I *urge* you to buy it."

A large black flag with a swastika was unfurled in the NPP group. The effect on the students was so shocking the quadrangle was momentarily gripped in silence. Lunz turned and looked at the flag but made no effort to stop it. He seemed happy to see it. Mona grasped my arm. "Oh, no," she uttered. "Oh, no!"

Three students plowed headlong into the NPP group and dove for the flag.

A student shouted, "*Hail Shitler! Hail Shitler, Hail Shitler!*" Soon, more students joined. The quadrangle filled with shouts of Hail Shitler. Students flooded into the NPP group. If it were not for the armbands of the NPP, it would have been difficult to know who was who.

"*Sieg Heil!*" a NPP member shouted. Others joined. "*Sieg Heil, Sieg Heil!*" The words rang across the quadrangle again and again.

"*Damn the Nazis! Damn the Nazis!*" a student shouted. "*All of you, go to hell!*"

Fighting continued. The quadrangle became a mass of students and the NPP attacking each other, fists swinging wildly. Police swarmed into the crowd but were too outnumbered to control the situation. A few students attempted to quell the madness. Most dove in and joined the fighting.

"Stop, stop!" Mona yelled. "Please! Stop!"

Lunz picked up the bullhorn and began shouting, "*Long live the NPP! Long live the NPP! The NPP will save you. Join the NPP.*" His words echoed through the quadrangle. He made no effort to control the chaos. His face was aglow in the thrill of the moment. It reminded me of the many encounters I had with him in my room—a grotesque blend of anger and joy that seemed to perpetually pour from some deep and eternal pit inside him. It was evident how ecstatic he was, as if pulling the strings of the NPP like mindless marionettes.

A second swastika flag appeared and then a third. More fighting broke out. An NPP member was shoved to the ground and kicked; he grabbed the leg of his assailant and pulled him down and the treatment was reversed in the clutch of the NPP. He shielded his face but was savagely attacked. Blood covered his face. I attempted to help him. Suddenly I felt a sharp pain. The left side of my shirt was saturated with purple-red blood. Students and NPP were locked in battle everywhere. Punches were thrown wildly. I was in a swirling hurricane of people filled with rage and spite. I had become separated from Mona. Students and NPP were brawling in an uncontrolled free-for-all. I felt a sharp pain in my side a second time. Grabbing instinctively for my flank, my palm dripped with blood. A brave female student threw a swastika flag on the ground and smeared it into the wet dirt and grass. The sharp snap of a gunshot echoed through the quadrangle. I froze, unsure where the sound came from. I hunted for Mona. The melee continued to get worse. Finally, Crocket snatched the bullhorn from Lunz and demanded peace. Little good it did until a phalanx of police plowed into the crowd and separated the groups. The students were ordered to immediately leave the quadrangle. The NPP was escorted off campus.

I heard Mona calling. As the crowd thinned, we came together. She looked at my blood-soaked shirt.

"Oh no! Oh no! Oh no! What happened?"

I pulled in a deep breath, feeling dizzy and weak. I shook my head. "I don't know." I hunched over, hands on my knees.

"Did you get shot?"

"I don't think so." I knew it was unlikely to be from a bullet. The NPP had to pass through metal detectors to get to the quadrangle.

Mona pulled my shirt up and shuddered. "It doesn't look good. How do you feel?"

"Not great."

We went to the health center where there was a line of students waiting to be treated for similar injuries.

"I knew this was going to happen," Mona said. "I knew it would. That low-life Krause Lunz should have known it, too. As soon as they started waving swastikas, I knew trouble was on its way. It's amazing that worse did not happen. They should throw Lunz out of Bradford once and for all."

I didn't tell her about the gunshot I heard. Enough bad news for now. I got to see the doctor after a long wait. He said it looked like a stab wound. From what he could tell it was not deep. A few stitches and a tetanus shot.

26

I did not expect to see Krause Lunz for quite a while. The semester would be over in a couple of months and from what Lunz told me he would be leaving Bradford—never to return. How many times had I wished that were true? Thus, I thought little if any about him other than when my hand subliminally passed across the still tender wound on my side. My time and energy were tied up with my writing classes, fun times with Mona, and the oppressive hours and days I spent writing my novel, a piece of work I knew to be little more than a crude and shabby beginner's attempt.

February slipped into March. Mona and I anxiously awaited the ensuing spring days that were destined to arrive. But this was New Hampshire and, as in Chicago, spring would not merely burst flamboyantly around us. It would come forth in sputtering starts and stops as it struggled to push back the cantankerous cold weeks of winter.

I remember the day well. I had just returned from class, had just set my backpack down, made a cup of tea, and had pulled my latest contribution to my manuscript from my desk. Reading what I had written did nothing to cheer me. But I would plug forward for an hour or so nonetheless. A paragraph, two para-graphs perhaps, and then set it aside for the day. I had a strange sense that the morning was about to be ravaged. My eyes landed on the doorway. There he was. Though unmistakably him, he had a hideous new addition to his appearance. On his upper lip, barely wider than his nose, was a black mustache. Hair dyed dark and angled across his forehead. Hitleresque to a tee. I wondered mo-mentarily if it was meant to be a sick joke. Realizing it wasn't, I turned my gaze to the window for a second as though Asmodeus had just entered my room, then turned to Lunz again.

"*Get the fuck out of here, Lunz. You are not welcome here!*"

"What anger. What's bugging Nicholas Schefield today?"

"*Get the fuck out!*" I said, waving an arm toward the door.

"A bright and beautiful day and Schefield is ruining it with another one of his tantrums. For Christ's sake, loosen up, dude. Perhaps a class in anger management is in order."

"*I said get the hell out of here!*"

"*Jesus!* What's chewing at you?"

"*You don't know?*"

"Okay, just a guess. Let me take a wild guess. Something to do with our rally." He watched my reaction. "Bing…go," he said gleefully. "I'm quite good at reading body language and I can tell Schefield is pissed."

"Fuck you, Lunz!"

"Haven't seen you in a while, Schefield. Thought I'd come over and get your take on our rally. Here's my take on it. Some people thought it got a little…what should I say…a little wild. That's what some thought. Well—"

"*Wild?* It was out of control. Which NPP rally were you at? The one I was at was a huge disaster…pure mayhem. A forum to spread hatred by that glorious NPP pack of neo-Nazi racists, and that neo-Nazi jackass you brought in to speak."

"Who? Crocket? Thought he slayed the crowd. The guy was savage. Calm, articulate, had his act together. Made his case in ways the kids could understand. What more could you want even from a yokel like Crockett? Have to say, I was damn gagged by the guy. You can tell already how eloquent he's going to be when he gets his chance at the podium on the floor of Congress."

I marveled at how Lunz always seemed so merry when he was tearing apart the NPP members he so ardently supported. A very strange love affair.

"That fucking rally of yours turned out exactly like everyone predicted. Nazi flags with swastikas on them. Damn disgusting!"

Lunz walked stiffly into the room, ignoring my comment. He rubbed his fingers over his mustache and checked to see if his hair was angled properly. "Ah…one or two flags," he finally conceded, discarding it with a shrug.

"I was glad to see them, if you want to know. The flags, I mean."

"Well, *that* slaps," Lunz said, struck by my comment.

"It spoke volumes about what your perverse group, the NPP, what it's really about. For a while I wondered if you were just a blowhard in search of attention. And even when you dropped that manifesto of yours on my desk, I was never totally convinced that you believed all the garbage in it. A part of me considered that you were one of those clowns who goes around irritating the shit out of people and loving every minute of it. I may not know much about human behavior, not like you seem to, but you don't have to be Sigmund Freud to have a sense of why people do what they do—"

"Christ almighty, spare me your analysis, Schefield." Lunz crunched his lips and cheeks into a curt bubble that amplified the effects of his foolish mustache and the hair that sloped across his forehead. A furious little Hitler, he was. "Whatever neuroses I *might* have had, I managed to exorcise on my own, no thanks to you know who. The rally was a winner for us, that's all that matters. We picked up a slew of new NPP members. Requests to join are still coming in. Yes, from right here at Bradford. More than we ever hoped for. See, even at a left-wing hovel like Bradford there are plenty of retards looking for something new to dig into. People in this country have the brains of amoebas. Told you that already a thousand times. And we got coverage on all the cable news stations, we made headway on all fronts. Stuff that in your meerschaum and smoke it."

"Don't be funny. You didn't make any progress," I said. "That's total fantasy. Total paranoid fantasy. Complete—"

"I told you, spare me your goddamn analysis. I could pick that little twig of brain of yours apart in two minutes, but I won't because despite the vast differences between you and me…" He stopped speaking for a second and then in a quieter voice said, "I used to think of you as a friend—"

I gagged. "Boy are we hallucinating! Not in a million years, Lunz. My friends do not despise people because of the color of their skin or because of their religion. I'm surprised Bradford didn't throw your ass out after what happened on the quad when you brought that raging bunch of NPP lunatics to campus." I showed Lunz the scar from the knife wound. "I wasn't the only one. There was a long line of us at the clinic with the same thing. A student was shot, damn near killed. I'm sure you heard about it. Or have you conveniently blotted that out of your mind?"

Lunz walked to the window as he had done scores of times before. "Not a peep from the administration. And by whatever means you got that little slit, it didn't come from one of us. We were unarmed. No guns, no knives. One hundred percent lean and clean. As for the student who got shot, yeah, I heard about it. Guy didn't die. He got shot in the leg. BFD. Hardly a serious wound. Likely from his own gun, in fact. I'm going to tell you something. You won't believe it, but it's true. Won't believe it because of that tight confirmation bias that rules your life." He glanced over his shoulder at me. "Know what confirmation bias is?"

"*Yes*, Lunz, I know what it is."

"Confirmation bias. It's when we cherry-pick what we want to believe. Pick only that which fits into our worldview."

"Don't insult me, Lunz. I told you I know what it is."

"Good for you. See, you have no way of knowing you got that cut of yours from one of the NPP. Could have been one of your own who skewered you. Didn't come from us. We were unarmed. No guns, no knives. But the fact is, all pinkos have a mega dose of confirmation bias. That's the fundamental difference between me and you, Schefield. That's what sets us apart. You need to put on your big-boy pants and start paying attention. I learned long ago how to cleanse my life of what others wanted me to believe and to fetch out the truth on my own. Unlike all you pinko twits, my life is governed by logic. This country is fast leaving people like you behind."

"Still a miracle someone did not get killed," I said.

"You're freaking hopeless," Lunz said. He readjusted his hair and thundered out.

27

Three days later, returning to my room after class, I found the door open and Krause Lunz sitting with his arms stretched over my desk, his face torn with anger.

"How the hell did you get into my room?" I demanded.

"*You mother fucker,*" he roared. "So this is what you've been up to." He held my manuscript, shaking it furiously. "*You sonuvabitch!* Writing about me. Is that it? Writing about us! About the NPP."

"What the hell are you talking about?" I said, stepping into the room. "And who the hell let you in here?"

"*You bastard—*"

"Give me that," I demanded. "It's none of your business what I do in my room. That has nothing to do with you."

Lunz's face was contorted, making his Hitler mustache appear both comical and grotesque. "You think I'm an imbecile? I read what you wrote. You're a mole for the FBI, sitting there at your goddamn desk recording everything that goes on around here. We've known all along that students were doing it but never knew who it was. *Now* I know. You're the dickhead who has been feeding them information."

"How the hell did you get in here?" I demanded again.

Lunz stood up and threw the manuscript at me. Pages sailed throughout the room. He started toward me with the eyes of someone who had been heavily into the bottle.

"*Get the hell out of here!*" I ordered. "*Now, or I'll call security.*"

"Go ahead, call fucking security…see what I care. I'm going to kill you," he said, coming around the desk and moving quickly toward me. "You sonuvabitch, Schefield." He dove at me and knocked me to the floor. I tried to grab him by the throat but was pinned down. He cocked his arm and swung wildly, missing me by inches. I jammed the butt of my palm into his chin. He took another broad swipe, this time landing his knuckles squarely on my jaw. Blood flowed into my mouth. "You bastard!" he kept yelling.

Adrenalin gushed through me. Finally getting him off, I pushed him against the floor and delivered three solid blows one after another to the side of his face. If it fazed him, you would never know it. With a burst of strength, he threw me on my back. I turned my head and managed to avoid his fist. He cocked back again and caught me on the jaw.

"You bastard!" he roared, grabbing my shoulders and slamming me repeatedly onto the floor. One, two, three, each time harder.

I pushed him away and jammed my fist into his throat. He coughed and gagged but kept after me. "You sonuvabitch! I'll kill you!" Again, his fist snapped across my jaw. His eyes were wide in rage.

With all my energy I got him off me and threw him on his back and unloaded two fast and hard shots to the side of his face.

Half a dozen people now gathered outside the door; two of

them pulled us apart.

"Get the hell out of here," I demanded, climbing to my knees and holding my lip. "And who the hell let you in here in the first place? Why were you rummaging through my desk?"

Lunz started for the door looking no worse for the wear. "Oh, go to hell. Ask Howie Berman," he said on his way out.

I sat in my chair, chin in my hands and got up and went to the bathroom to see what was left of me. My lip was purple, puffy, and swollen. My teeth, gratefully, were intact. I ran cold water over a washcloth, wrung it out, returned to the room, leaned back and bathed my lip.

Pages of my novel were spewed everywhere. Just as well. It was becoming a genuine curse. First Mona, now Lunz. Was this the Muse giving me a final curtain call, telling me to scrap my writing and save my soul—and body—before it was too late? *Jesus H. Christ*, I thought, closing my eyes and pressing the washcloth to my lip.

A text came in on my phone. Without looking, I knew it was from Mona. I would get back to her later. I pressed the cloth to my lip. My body was still drenched in adrenalin. I sat as quietly as possible waiting for my breathing to slow. I did not want to look around the room, did not want to see the pages of what I had written spread hither and yon.

"Nicholas?" Mona looked at the room and came over and knelt next to me. "*What happened?*" she gasped. "Oh, *mon amour*, what happened? Are you okay? Who did this? Are you okay?"

Before I could say a word, she said, "Did Lunz do this?"

I nodded.

Mona lifted the cloth from my lip and gasped again.

"It's all right...it looks worse than it is," I said, slurring my words.

"Let's get you to the doctor. You should have someone look at your lip. It doesn't look good at all."

"It's all right. I'm fine…I'll be all right."

"Tell me what happened."

I rested my forehead in my palms and groaned. "I don't feel like talking about it."

"Tell me what happened. Did you get my text?"

I nodded. "Uh-huh."

"We were planning to go over to Salento in Huntington Wells. Me and Jennifer Rubinstein. I thought you might want to go. When you didn't reply, I got concerned." She took the washcloth and went to the bathroom and came back with a fresh cold one. "I think you should lie down a while. Your lip doesn't look good."

"I'm fine," I said.

"Lie on the bed for a few minutes…okay?"

"I think I'll be better if I don't."

"Will you tell me what happened?"

"I'd rather not get into it. Let's just get the hell out of here for a while. Get Jennifer. I'll go with you to Salento. Any place but here."

Mona drew in a slow breath. "All right, if you want…all right."

"Yes, I'd rather go."

"I'll tell Jennifer to meet us there."

I got up and rinsed my face and changed my shirt. We left the dorm and crossed campus and went to Huntington Wells. The café had the usual mix of students and townies. A song by Wilco was playing when we walked in. We sat at a table on the edge of the room.

Jennifer arrived minutes later. She looked at me. "Nick? What *happened?*"

I gave her a brief rundown, about as much as I told Mona, which wasn't much. And then left it at that.

"How did Lunz get in your room?" Jennifer asked.

"Berman, pwobably," I mumbled, as best I could with my swollen lips. "The master key, no doubt."

"Sounds like the kind of crap Berman would do. He's pretty much a creep like Lunz. I think he's a henchman for that organization of his. I'm pretty certain he's the suss that's been snooping around in the dorm rooms. Him and Lunz, too."

"According to Lunz, he's part of the NPP," I said.

"No surprise, he's been sucking up to Lunz for quite a while," Jennifer said. "I know one of them was in our room a while back. Holly told me she was sure of it, but I thought it finally stopped. Then last week I realized someone was in again. Lunz or Berman, one of them. Maybe both. Who knows? I'm getting real fed up with it!" She looked quizzically at me. "But I don't get it. Why would they want to go into your room?"

"Oh, you know, like I said, Lunz used to come in and dump all kinds of political garbage on me. The guy is paranoid. Needs some long visits with those parents of his, the shrinks. He comes in and tells me everything he's up to. He thinks I care, but I don't. Lately, he's been talking a lot about the FBI and the Deep State, paranoid junk like that. I let him blab on for a while and then run him out." I rubbed my hand across my chin. "When he was in my room, or maybe when Berman was there, whoever it was, he found a writing book of mine in my desk. Lunz freaked out. Accused me of writing about him and being a mole for the FBI. He claimed there are people on campus who follow everything the NPP does, that they're doing the dirty work for the FBI. The guy is batshit crazy."

"I thought Lunz was planning to leave Bradford soon. That's what Berman told me," Jennifer said.

"He's working on some NPP junk and might go to Washington to work in the office of that imbecile Horace Crockett. Remember Crockett…the goon Lunz brought here for his rally?"

"What's this country coming to? Mona said. "It's getting worse and worse all the time. Maybe we should go live in France. I managed to learn a little French over the years from my father. We could live in Paris. You could write there. Become like the great writers after the First World War. Won't that be fun?"

"Well, my Fwench sucks," I slurred.

Mona laughed. "See, it's getting better already."

Jennifer said, "And I can move to Paris and study medicine at the Sorbonne."

Back in my room, I gathered the mess Lunz had created and clipped the pages of my writing into a shabby notebook. It did little for my pride.

Despite it all, I continued to work daily on my novel. I tallied the number of words—sixty-three thousand in all. Far more than I thought I would achieve. The character crafted after Krause Lunz was indeed an emotional wreck.

28

Hoping to avoid Lunz at all cost, I spent much of my time in Mona's room, though at one point I ran into Howie Berman in the hallway. I jammed a finger onto his chest and told him I knew Lunz had been in my room, but that Lunz told me Berman was the actual perp. Berman pathetically denied it. "Why would I do that?" he said almost softly, emoting a look of contrition as if admitting culpability for what had happened. I warned him in all caps that he damn well better stay the fuck out of my room.

It was late in the day. I was in my room trying to wrap up a storm of assignments that needed to be completed by the end of the semester. Figuring Lunz would not be so bold as to make an appearance, I left the door open and was working feverishly when there in the doorway stood Krause Lunz. Before he moved an inch, I was out of my chair.

"Schefield, Schefield…hold on," Lunz said in a faintly compliant tone, taking a step back. "Give me a minute."

"I don't have a minute and I have no plans to listen to your bullshit so get the hell!"

He pulled in a short breath and exhaled. "Okay, I know

you're ticked about what happened. I know. I know."

"*Ticked?*"

"Okay, okay, I get it. Would it help if I apologized?"

"Lunz, you're one screwed up sonuvabitch."

"Uh-huh."

"So, what the hell are you doing in here then? You need to go get your head checked. That should be easy to do. You've got some very big issues, dude. Big issues!"

Lunz simpered as if he knew it to be true. "Yeah, yeah, yeah. When I was in here and blew up…well—"

"Everything you do around here turns into a disaster. I'm not looking for apologies. Best thing is if you don't come around here. Get it? You're trouble. Pure trouble. Slum your way out of here once and for all and stay out."

Lunz took a small step into the room.

"*Lunz?*"

He held his hand up as if to say, give me a minute. "Okay, I was a little beside myself when we…when the blowout between us happened—"

"*Blowout?* You should have seen what my lip looked like. First I get stabbed at that goddamn rally of yours and then you come in here and—"

Lunz shoved his hands into his pockets. "Can you listen for a minute?"

I waited, not sure what his motives were. As he started to speak, I said, "Still damn pissed you were snooping around my room."

Lunz shook his head. "It wasn't me. It was Berman. He brought me the, you know, your…."

"Oh, dump it all on Berman now. Is that it? Berman told me

it was all *your* doing. I suppose he's the one who went nuts and cracked my face."

"I don't have keys to the rooms."

"No, but your stooge Berman does."

"Sure. He's a stooge…and a snoop. But he doesn't feed me information. Sometimes, he dumps something on my desk. Like the, uh…the stuff you wrote, I mean. I didn't ask him to do that. He brought it to me like a cat that snares a robin in the front yard. Berman is a creep, a hopeless creep. He uses that key of his to poke around in the rooms. He gets his jollies that way, if you know what I mean. The guy doesn't have a lot of friends."

"Looks to me like he has one."

"Ah, shit, he just latched on to me a long time ago when he learned my parents are shrinks. He'll be heading to medical school soon. He's knocking on the door of a bunch of places and he'll probably get into all of them. He wants to be a shrink." Lunz let out a sad sorrowful laugh. "He'll be a damn good one, being as screwed up as he is." He tried to laugh again but it fell flat. "Remember? Remember what I said? People become shrinks to rake all the demons out of their lives. I have firsthand evidence of this. Could write a bloody dissertation on it. That's what you learn when you're raised by two nut jobs."

"Christ almighty, Lunz, is there anyone on this planet you respect?"

Lunz shrugged. "So…are we still, you know…friends?"

"*FRIENDS! FRIENDS!*"

"Lunz, you're a racist, a misogynist, a bigot, a xenophobe, a chauvinist, a Nazi, a white supremacist. What else? A…"

This brought a ghost of a smile to Lunz's face. As though he knew it to be true. As if they were monikers he wore proudly. He made a sign of the cross, looked to the ceiling, tapped his chest, and said, "Bless me Father, for I have sinned, *mea culpa, mea culpa, mea maximum culpa.*"

"Get the hell out of here, Lunz!"

He looked at me in the queerest way. As though he truly believed we were friends. There was sadness in his face of the kind I had never seen before. He started to speak but said nothing. A layer of icy silence drew across the room until he turned and took to the door. His footsteps faded as he walked down the hall.

I got up and went to the window. The last remains of a morning snowfall caused the lights from the buildings to glisten on the ground. Earlier in the day Mona and I planned an evening rendezvous. There was nothing more perfect in this world I could imagine than a night with her. I turned the lights down in the room and sat in my soft chair and dozed off.

29

The semester rolled to an end. Mona, as you might expect, did well in her classes. I struggled through mine. It was the first time in my life that I had only a modicum of success in return for my labored efforts. Worse yet, my novel, now nearly completed, was little more than dreadful. I cringed as I read through it. If nothing else, I learned that it would be many years before I produced anything of worth. It did not matter. My desire to work for the State Department had vanished, as did any vague belief that a stethoscope or scalpel was in my future. I knew what I was going to do with my life and I knew it would be a long hard slog. If it takes years to be a doctor, years to be a good diplomat maybe, what's wrong with paying the dues that are needed to be a good writer? I looked at two quotes from Hemingway I had pinned to the wall. Quotes I viewed frequently.

"The first draft of anything is shit."
"It's none of their business that you have to learn how to write. Let them think you were born this way."

Perhaps Mona's impromptu suggestion that we move to Paris

was not such a bad idea. Lord knows, I had enough money from my father's estate to keep us in baguettes and croissants for a long while. We could get a flat in the Latin Quarter, make new friends, Mona would become fluent in French in no time and I might even be able to clumsily croak out a few words. I would get a beret and a pair of wire-rimmed glasses like James Joyce. We would drink beer and wine and aperitifs in the cafés in the evenings with friends and maybe take the TGV on weekends to Lyon, the true culinary capital of France, where we would dine as elegantly as the French do on *Sole Meunière* and *Coq au Vin* and share a bottle of *Bourgogne* from Pommard or a delicate and delightful *Muscadet* from the Loire Valley. Perhaps, there in France, I would find a muse that would be more kind to me. As Hemingway said in the last line of *The Sun Also Rises*, "Isn't it pretty to think so."

I was sitting in my room working diligently on my final writing assignment. Despite purported sightings of Lunz on campus, Holly Clarke was told he had cleaned out his room, packed up, and left for good. Off for green pastures far, far from Bradford, I assumed. To Washington or out pulverizing another election with one of his NPP candidates.

A noise came from down the hall. I listened for a moment, then got up. Looking out my door, I saw students and security clustering outside Lunz's room. I walked part way down the hall. Security pushed people aside as a stretcher was wheeled into Lunz's room. Minutes later it came out with a tarp-covered body.

Mona and Holly Clarke and Jennifer Rubinstein came over. "What happened?" I asked.

"It's Lunz," Jennifer Rubinstein said in a low voice. "He apparently committed suicide."

I was shocked but in a strange way not surprised. I found no words to add to what I had heard. I watched as the stretcher rolled down the hall, as Lunz left the dorm for the last time.

Later that evening I learned some details of Lunz's death. He had hanged himself. He was found by Howie Berman along with a note he left.

Was I sorry that Lunz was no longer part of the family of man on this planet? Not for a second. I remembered how, after the catastrophe sparked by the neo-Nazis in Charlottesville, Donald Trump said there were some good people on both sides. He was wrong, and all sensible people knew it. Krause Lunz was not an aberration. A fallen angel. I knew that the hatred he possessed was real, that it coursed through every fiber of his body, that there was nothing good in his heart when it came to his worldview.

A few days later, Howie Berman confided to Jennifer Rubinstein what was in the note Lunz left behind. It said that he knew his mother is Jewish and that although he had known this his whole life, he could not live with the knowledge of that. And could not live with the fact that he also is Jewish. He despised his father for marrying a Jew. It was a shocking revelation, but as with most everything I came to know about Krause Lunz in the time I had been around him, he never learned to change, to adapt, to accept those parts of life that troubled him. Yet another example of how he was unable to live with the cards he had been dealt.

I had matured during my nine months at Bradford. I had become less tolerant of the anger and hatred that fills the souls of some people. And though I was still in many ways a passive person, I knew I would never again tolerate such people.

The school year ended. In many ways it had been a tormenting one due almost entirely to the perpetual unsolicited visits from Krause Lunz. To that was added the loss of my father whom I never knew very well. But like most parts of life, there was a blend of sunshine with the darkness.

Monique Dubois, Monique Dubois.